Biffy Ferguson and the
Cheese Mice from Mars

Enjoy Jacob

Robert A Peter

Biffy Ferguson and the Cheese Mice from Mars

ROBERT A PETER

authorHOUSE®

AuthorHouse™ UK
1663 Liberty Drive
Bloomington, IN 47403 USA
www.authorhouse.co.uk
Phone: 0800.197.4150

Published by AuthorHouse 07/23/2015

ISBN: 978-1-5049-8757-8 (sc)
ISBN: 978-1-5049-8756-1 (e)

For Biffy, a wonderful cat

CHAPTER 1

A Nasty Surprise

Biffy stopped suddenly, causing a bit of a nose-to-tail pile-up. There was a muffled "Ummpff!" as Robbie walked straight into Biffy's rear end. This was closely followed by Marple piling into Robbie. "*Wotcha!*" shouted Marple in surprise.

"What's up now?" asked Marple, unceremoniously spitting out dog hair.

"And where do you three think you're going?" asked a rude and disagreeable yet rather familiar voice.

Looking round from behind Biffy, Robbie saw two large black cats standing in their way. Marple then peered round from behind Robbie. "O-o-Oh!" he said, catching on to what was happening up front.

"I thought Sable and I made it clear after our last …" At this point the black cat who was doing all the talking up until now paused as if savouring what he was going to say next and feeling really pleased with himself. Grinning nastily, he ended his sentence with "meeting" and sniggered in a low hissing way that sounded a bit like a faulty kettle trying to boil.

"You don't scare me, Panther!" said Robbie, coming up to support Biffy. Biffy said nothing.

"That's odd," said the black cat called Sable. "That's exactly what I thought we were doing."

Sable then slowly lifted up a paw, and five razor-sharp claws sprang out like flick knives in a gangster film. Flexing each individual claw menacingly, he said, "You now have two choices." Pausing for effect, he continued, "Go back the way you came and leave our territory!"

"Or?" interrupted Biffy rather coolly, considering the current situation.

"You lose an eye," said Panther, casually flexing his claws.

Biffy slowly sat down and thought, *How come such a peaceful start to the day has turned so complicated so soon?* and for a brief moment forgot their immediate danger and dreamily remembered the start of the day.

Chapter 2

A Day Like Any Other

It was a day like any other, or so thought Biffy Ferguson. Biffy had just woken up after having a long and well-deserved sleep. What was so particularly well-deserved about this sleep only Biffy's inner cat would ever know.

Stretching out his front paws and pointing his posterior at the sky in that luxurious way that only cats can, known to all cats as the "Salute with the bum", it occurred to Biffy that life is good. The only major decision he faced was whether to go back to sleep or have a quick groom. As he was not in the mood for any grooming, an activity that seemed to have lost its magic over the years, he decided to go back to sleep.

Biffy Ferguson was a large, 8-year-old tabby cat with an odd orange tip on the end of his tail that he was rather proud of. Biffy thought of himself as a sophisticated yet down-to-earth cat about town. His colouring actually resembled quite closely the markings of a Scottish wildcat, with those beautiful dark rings on the tail, except for the orange tip, of course!

Biffy officially lived at number 3 Round Oak Crescent, in the historic Somerset village of Cheddar. Cheddar is a rather delightful and – up till now – peaceful part of southwest England. Biffy, however, like most cats, also had at least three alternative homes – or to be blunt, places where he could go to get another meal.

You may wonder if the inventor of the cat flap knew just what a revolutionary effect it would have on the evolution of the domestic cat's social life. Soon the sound of the cat flap opening and closing, instead of being met with the phrase "Ah! Here's Tiddles!" was replaced with the phrase "Now who the heck is it this time?"

Biffy always found it amusing the way humans think they owned particular cats, while in fact cats know that they are owned by no one and are their own masters.

CHAPTER 3

Preparations for Conquest

Meanwhile, out in space, a small fleet of spaceships, having travelled all the way from the red planet Mars, had managed to sneak up as far as the moon, totally unobserved by anybody on Earth, mainly because no one on Earth was looking in the right direction at the time. Also, because the invaders were mice, their spaceships were rather small compared with human spaceships. However, compared with earth-born mice, Martian mice are rather large, mainly because Martian gravity is only about one third that of Earth. In fact Martian mice are about the size of a large earth rat. Even so, the entire fleet could still fit into a double domestic garage.

It all started a few months earlier when, as one of the world's first and greatest science fiction writers, H. G. Wells, put it: "This world was being watched keenly and closely by intelligences greater than man's." However, Mr Wells was not aware that this intelligence had a cheese fixation and a tendency to squeak a lot.

Mars can be as far away from Earth as 200,000,000 miles, a distance that is just over twice the distance from the earth to the sun, which on average is about 93,000,000 miles. This distance, as all budding young junior astronomers know, is called an astronomical unit. Even at its closest distance of about 49 million miles, which is just over half the expanse between the earth and the sun, this still creates certain disadvantages when it comes to dropping buy for a visit or for the occasional planetary conquest.

This, however, did not stop General Squeakcheesy from dreaming of the day when Earth would be theirs. After all, every mouse on Mars knew that Earth was made of green cheese. But to return to the thoughts of Mr H. G. Wells about the occupants of the red planet, he wrote: "Slowly and surely they drew their plans against us."

General Squeakcheesy had laboured long and hard over his secret plans for the conquest of Earth, and after many sleepless nights and long hours of study and planning, they went something like this: Get to Earth, grab all the cheese, and then get out quick.

Never since the siege of Troy had such a splendid and masterly plan been devised – more glorious than the battle orders for Waterloo, bigger even than the plans for D-Day, or so thought the general.

The first cheese lord, Lord Gorgonzola (who was known affectionately by the Martian populace as the Big Cheese) thought that General Squeakcheesy was an idiot. Nevertheless, he gave his consent to this daring scheme, being rather partial to the odd bit of cheese himself. After all, if it failed, who would ever know? And he would be rid of a rather annoying twit.

Chapter 4

An Exploding Bush

While the cheese mice from Mars prepared to attack, Biffy woke up again and pondered his next move for the day – if he was going to move at all, that is. *Ah decisions, decisions*, thought Biffy, rather sagely.

Suddenly there was a commotion from behind the rhododendrons at the bottom of the garden.

"Why can't we just come in through the front gate like everybody else?" said a familiar voice.

"Because it's not a front gate day," replied another familiar voice.

Oh no, I have a bad feeling about this! thought Biffy, sitting up to greet the intruders.

There was a sort of muffled yelp, followed by several snappings, crunchings, rustlings, and what can only be described as sounding like an angry bush fighting a wasp.

"Stop pushing, will you?" shouted an exasperated voice.

"Oh get on with it. We haven't got all day!" said the second waspishly.

"You try and get on with it with one branch up your nose and another trying to get acquainted with your rear end."

Suddenly there was a quiet but explosive ejection of a tangle of annoyed fur and legs.

Trying to remain coolly aloof to all the excitement and the slowly disentangling fur ball, Biffy recognised his friends Mr Marple, the large ginger tom from two doors down, and Robbie, the West Highland terrier from across the road.

Mr Marple, who was just called Marple by his friends, happened to be owned by two people who were huge Agatha Christie fans. They also had a goldfish called Poirot and a budgie called Agatha.

Robbie was rumoured to be a distant cousin of Greyfriars Bobby, the famous nineteenth-century Edinburgh dog who stayed by his master's grave and was looked after by the local people in recognition of his loyalty. Biffy thought that Robbie had started this rumour himself.

While Robbie trotted forward to greet Biffy, Marple was trying to delicately remove a small branch that had somehow become entangled in the fur of his hind quarters. This was proofing quite difficult because he was trying to do it without anyone noticing. Having achieved this almost impossible task, he trotted over to join the other two.

"Hello Biff, mate, how is it going?" asked Marple.

"It was going rather well until rudely interrupted by an exploding bush!" replied Biffy in what he hoped was his most indignant manner.

"Great!" said Robbie. "Me and Marple …"

"Marple and I," corrected Biffy.

Slightly miffed at the interruption, Robbie continued stiffly, raising his voice slightly as he corrected the start to his announcement.

"*Marple and I* …" whereupon he paused briefly to give Biffy a searching look before continuing, "were planning on going down to the reservoir, you know, down at the bottom of Holwell Lane."

"And what were you planning to do once you get there?" asked Biffy sceptically.

"Oh you know, do a bit of chilling out."

"You mean doing nothing," said Biffy.

"Yep," replied Marple, joining in the conversation.

"Well I can do that perfectly well here without all that exertion," said Biffy. He lay down again, saying through a yawn, "I'm just going to go back to sleep." Then he hunkered down for another forty winks.

"This is no time for slouching!" announced Robbie. "If you're not in the mood for loafing, then there's glory and trumpets and really wild times to be had!"

Biffy thought hopefully, *Oh brother, maybe if I keep on ignoring them they will go away.* But deep down he just knew that some form of exertion was inescapably looming on the horizon.

Resignedly, Biffy got up slowly and had another long stretch. "You must show me how to do that," said Robbie.

Biffy just looked at him aloofly and said, "Come back tomorrow as a cat and I will." Then he turned, swishing Robbie in the face with his tail.

"Come on, then, let's go down to the reservoir," said Biffy, heading for the front of the house.

They left by the front gate this time, trotting in single file round the crescent on to Round Oak Grove that led to Round Oak Road. They had been following the grove for only a few minutes when Biffy said, without looking round, "We will probably bang into Tia. She is usually on her rounds around this time of day, and we should ask her to come with us."

"Oh, that large German shepherd from the old Manor house," said Marple.

"Yes, lovely dog when you get to know her," said Biffy.

"Great idea," said Robbie.

"You know we have to cross that busy road that goes to Axbridge?" observed Marple.

Biffy stopped and turned, saying: "Actually, we don't have to cross the road at all. We can use the Rye Stream culvert."

Robbie looked confused for a moment until Biffy said, "Remember it passes under the road and comes out just behind that row of houses on the other side of the road?"

"Won't that be a bit wet?" asked Marple in a concerned voice.

"Not at this time of year," replied Biffy. "It should be down to a trickle, allowing us to walk along the side where it's usually dry all summer."

The three friends quickly crossed over Round Oak Road, looking carefully first to make sure it was safe to cross, and snuck under the hedge into the nearest garden.

CHAPTER 5

Tia Saves the Day

Biffy awoke suddenly from his daydream. You will remember that we left Biffy and his friends being confronted by two nasty black cats.

"Are you listening to me?" asked the black cat called Panther.

Biffy stared him straight in the eye and replied, "Well I tried not to, but some of it still got through."

A look of pure hatred grew across the face of Biffy's opponent.

Any second now, thought Biffy, who had just heard a familiar noise, faint but unmistakable, from the other side of the hedge. There was a scrabbling sound from underneath the hedge where Biffy and his friends had come under just a few minutes previously. The head of a large, long-haired German shepherd appeared from below the hedge.

"Hello, Biff. I thought that was your scent there. Hey, what's going on here then?" said Tia suddenly realising that something was up.

"Well, Tia, these two rat-bags were just about to rearrange my face."

Tia squeezed the rest of her not unsubstantial bulk from under the hedge.

"Is that so?" she asked, looking at the two black cats menacingly.

The other black cat, the one called Sable, took a timorous step forward and said, "This is none of your business, dog."

Biffy smiled and thought, not the cleverest thing to say to a proud German shepherd bitch.

Tia suddenly lurched towards the cheeky cat, barking madly. Just in time, the cat dived under Tia's body and sped off under the garden hedge and away down the road like a record-breaking express train and making about as much noise.

The other cat had quickly sized up the situation and swiftly climbed up the nearest tree. He sat, perched in the crook of a large tree limb, staring down at Tia, who was running round the base of the tree, barking fiercely and occasionally leaping up against the tree trunk, trying to get closer to the black cat.

"I'll get you for this!" spat Panther.

"Oh yeah?" shouted Biffy up into the branches. "Looks like you'll be spending the rest of the day admiring the view from up there!"

Tia sat on her haunches and licked her lips. "How long would you like me to keep this up, Biffy mate?" she enquired coolly.

"Oh, a couple of hours will do, I expect," answered Biffy with a smile.

"No problemo! Sounds like fun," said Tia.

Panther hissed and spat at the group gathered at the bottom of the tree. The only effect of this was to send Tia barking madly round the tree again.

Biffy turned to Robbie and Marple and said, "Well, we shouldn't have any trouble from those two for a while. Shall we continue?"

So the trio walked quickly through the garden and out through a gap in the rear fence to where the stream flowed just behind the houses.

CHAPTER 6

The Squeakascope

While Biffy, Robbie, and Marple were heading for the reservoir, out in space General Squeakcheesy had ordered the fleet of six spaceships to hide behind the moon until he had studied the latest report about the earth from Professor Cleversqueak, Mars's chief scientist.

The report, based on telescopic observation of the earth–moon system, indicated that when the moon was full as seen from Earth, the earth would be in nightfall on the side facing the moon, so ideal for a sneak landing by the invasion force.

The mice had also been monitoring the earth's radio signals, especially the BBC, and by pure chance had overheard a local news report from BBC Somerset about, of all things, a cheese festival in an earth village with the name of Cheddar. The mice could hardly believe their luck! So the stories were true: There is lots of cheese on Earth.

The general looked up at the clock, which had been set to earth time. It was ten o'clock in the morning in the UK.

"OK, in about eleven hours it will start to get dark over the target area." The general was addressing his invasion command group, which consisted of himself (of course), his second in command Lieutenant Fondue, and the captains of the other five ships of the invasion fleet.

"I'm going to take the flagship round to the other side of the moon and take a quick look at our proposed landing site with the squeakascope. Once we have some pictures of the site, we can prepare the landing plan. Meet me back here in three hours." The mice captains all saluted and left to return to their ships.

The flagship and the rest of the fleet had been coated with a thin layer of grey moon dust using special space glue. The dust had been collected by Professor Cleversqueak on a previous expedition some years before. It was hoped that the dust covering would prevent the metal ship from reflecting sunlight and so make it invisible against the moon's surface.

Due to the current position of the moon in its orbit around the earth, the moon would be half full as seen from Europe. The flagship would therefore have to travel round to the lunar terminator, which is the division between the day side and the night side on the moon, in order to observe the target area in full daylight.

As an added precaution against observation, the general had ordered the flagship's pilot to hug the surface of the moon as closely as possible. So the pilot, Space Pilot Stilton, brought the ship down to a few hundred meters above the moon's surface and started to hug the rugged contours of the lunar landscape as they travelled around to the other side of the moon to find a suitable crater from which to observe the earth.

The general keenly observed the lunar ground features as they passed by. He looked through one of the forward portholes where he could also keep at least one eye on the blue and green marble that was the earth as it slowly appeared over the moon's horizon.

"It looks rather beautiful, don't you think sir?" commented Lieutenant Fondue, who was looking at the earth over the general's shoulder.

"Rather delicious," replied the general, thinking about all the cheese that they were about to capture.

Once they arrived at the terminator, the ship travelled parallel with it to get the earth into a better position for observation.

"OK, Pilot, keep going until the earth is a good height above the horizon, then find a good crater to land in," said the general.

"Aye, aye!" answered the pilot as he concentrated on the controls of the ship. After about an hour the pilot exclaimed, "Crater coming up!"

"OK, take her in and land in the middle, nice and easy," replied the general, who was still staring at the earth out of his porthole.

Space Pilot Stilton carefully brought the ship to a halt, just hovering over the middle of the crater. Then, while carefully manoeuvring her to avoid the crater's central peak, he lowered her down to the surface. As soon as the ship touched the surface, the pilot killed the engines. There was a slight jar as the ship's landing struts, which had been cleverly incorporated into the spaceship's tail fins, absorbed the impact of landing.

"Nice landing, Stilton!" commented the general.

"Thank you, sir," replied the pilot, saluting.

All was quiet in the ship's control room except for a slightly annoying, tinny, jingling sound with occasional blurts of hissing. The general turned to face his second in command and said in an annoyed voice, "Fondue, will you stop listening to that infernal device while you are on duty?"

"*What*?" shouted the general's second in command, who quickly turned red and took off his headphones. "Sorry, General, it's the latest Mouse Player Three. All the young mice on Mars are using them."

The general looked at Lieutenant Fondue scornfully and said, "Well, unless you want to walk the 49,000,000 miles back to join them, I would put it away."

Fondue went even redder and said, "Yes General, sorry General."

"What on Mars are you listing to anyway? Sounds like racket to me," said the general.

The lieutenant looked up from putting his music player away in a pocket and said, "It's Twiggy Star Blast and the Spiders from Earth."

"Twiggy what? Oh never mind," said the general, irritated.

He then turned to the communications officer, Ensign Loudsqueak, and commanded, "Turn on the squeakascope, and let's have a look at the landing site."

The communications officer started pushing buttons on a small keypad in his control panel that was located at the back of the command bridge of the ship. A large screen slowly descended from a hidden panel in the ceiling and flickered to life. Meanwhile, outside in the cold lunar daylight, a small hatch slid open in the smooth skin of the ship on the side facing the earth, revealing a telescope-like tube underneath.

Just above the open hatch was a shiny nameplate with large gold letters that said *R. S. Zulupapalulu*. Underneath, in smaller print, was the motto "In Cheese We Trust" The squeakascope tube slowly extended itself and moved until it pointed at the small blue and green planet that we call home.

The image of the earth as seen from space appeared on the large video screen inside the control bridge of the ship. The general put his paw inside his uniform jacket and produced a large piece of folded paper.

"This is a map of the earth that our scientists drew for me before we left Mars. It's based on months of careful telescopic observations." He carefully unfolded the paper and spread it on the small table that occupied the centre of the control bridge.

Lieutenant Fondue drew closer and stared at the unfolded sheet. With a puzzled yet amused look on his face, he said, "Sir, this is a recipe for cheese dip."

The general snatched the sheet away and, clearing his throat noisily, hurriedly put it back in his inside pocket. He quickly produced another sheet from the same hiding place and said, "This is the map."

Lieutenant Fondue knew better than to make any further comment about the matter and looked down at the unfolded map. The map consisted of a roughly drawn outline of the British Isles and part of northern Europe.

"It's not very detailed," commented the Lieutenant.

Looking over his shoulder, the pilot whispered, "That dip recipe would be more useful."

The lieutenant stifled a small laugh.

"What was that?" said the general, looking up.

"Nothing, General. The pilot was just suggesting that we dip the lights to view the screen better."

"Hrrumph! No, the light's fine!" said the general, clearing his throat again and giving the pilot a funny look.

The general took a pencil and pointed at the southwest of England on the map. He said, "Right. The village of

Cheddar is somewhere here. We can use the radio tracker to zero in on the location of the village."

Ensign Loudsqueak looked up from his controls and said, "Excuse me, General, but how do we know that the radio transmission is coming from that village and not some larger settlement?"

The general smiled and said, "Don't worry, the last broadcast that we monitored said that there was to be a special outside broadcast from the village on the day of the cheese festival. All we need to do is pick it up and zoom in on it."

"I will get right on it," said Ensign Loudsqueak.

The communications officer started punching buttons and turning dials on his control panel while carefully watching a small video display. The display showed a bright green wavy line that danced about the black screen. The wave started to smooth out and then straightened suddenly.

"Got it!" exclaimed Loudsqueak, just as the crackling static that had been coming from the screen seconds before changed into a posh English voice.

"Well, that was the weather. And now over to Dan with our special outside broadcast unit at the cheese festival in Cheddar."

"Thanks, John. Everything here in the lovely and historical village of Cheddar in the heart of Somerset is going splendidly." There was more static crackling. Then the voice came back. "The festival is being held under canvas in the grounds of the Kings of Wessex School." Again the reception was lost to static for a few seconds. "And the whole community is looking forward to …" The voice was once again lost in a static hiss.

"Can't you do something about that?" shouted the general.

"Sorry sir, it's the earth's ionosphere doing funny things to the radio waves."

"Well get the damn ionosphere the heck off the air, and get that broadcast back" roared the general, turning purple.

Loudsqueak sort of ducked behind his screen muttering something about not being able to change the laws of physics.

Just then, the reception cleared again, and the voice said, "… what may well turn out to be the world's largest cheese festival …"

The entire crew on board the Martian flagship stopped what they were doing and gasped. Many of them were mouthing the words they had just heard: "World's largest cheese festival!"

The voice came back one last time before the signal was lost for good. "Our broadcast vans are right inside the grounds, not far from the main marquee. Looks like cheese for supper, John."

The general broke the silence. "Well, mice, this is it! We've struck the mother lode."

He turned to the communications officer and said, "Loudsqueak, get that location locked into the computer. *It's cheese time!*" He shouted the last three words, getting quite carried away with the excitement of it all. The communications officer quickly got to work on his control panel.

"Location locked in, General."

The general came a bit closer to the video screen and said, "OK, let's zoom in. Maximum magnification!"

"Yes, sir," replied the ensign as he pushed buttons and keys on his control panel.

Unfortunately, each keystroke, button push, or any other operation made on the communications control panel made an annoyingly loud squeaking sound, something like: squeak, squeak, squeak, pause, then squeak, squeak, squeak.

The general, who in all the excitement of the last fifteen minutes had all but forgotten the annoying communications panels sound effects, said in exasperation, "Can't you do something about that squeaking, Loudsqueak?"

Ensign Loudsqueak looked quite offended and said, "But sir, we're mice."

The general's face turned a sort of purple colour, and he yelled, "I am very well aware of that fact, you idiot!"

He then composed himself and said in a more restrained voice, "I was referring to the irritating noise you produce every time you press a damn button."

"Oh that, sir. Sorry, sir."

The general came over to the young ensign and glared at him. "*Well*?" he shouted.

Loudsqueak looked down at his shoes and shuffled his feet in embarrassment, muttering, "It's built into the electronics of the communications computer. We can't do anything about it until we get back to Mars." He added lamely, "I think the designers thought it was funny. That's probably how the squeakascope got its name."

"I'll give them funny when I get back. I want it reprogrammed and renamed the never-squeak-again-a-scope," said the general. Returning his attention to the screen, he said, "Now get that image zoomed, Ensign."

"Yes, sir. Right away, sir!" said Loudsqueak, turning a large blue dial all the way round until it stopped. The image suddenly rushed forward and blurred.

"Arrgh!" exclaimed the general. "That always makes me dizzy."

"Nothing new there, then," whispered Lieutenant Fondue to the pilot.

Slowly the image cleared, revealing a typical English village as seen from a low-flying aeroplane, with lots of rooftops and gardens.

"Hmm, too close, take her back a few stops!"

The communications officer turned the blue dial back three clicks, and the screen blurred again for a second, then refocused again, this time showing the entire village and surrounding countryside.

"That's better. We need to find a suitable landing site. Let's see what we have," said the general.

CHAPTER 7

A Trip to the Reservoir

While the general and his fellow mice studied the area around the village in order to find a suitable landing site, Biffy and his friends made their way along the side of the stream towards the culvert that went under the road.

When the three friends got to the entrance of the culvert, they found that Biffy had been right: There was a clear, dry path right through to the other end.

"Come on, then," said Biffy, trotting into the darkened tunnel while the others followed behind reluctantly.

"It's a bit dirty," said a rather worried Robbie.

"Not to say draughty," said Marple.

"And yet you did," replied Biffy, who had stopped just inside the culvert entrance. Turning to his friends, he said, "If you would rather play catch with the traffic, you're welcome to go up and over the road instead."

Biffy's voice was almost drowned out by the roar of a passing tipper truck speeding along the road above them.

"OK, but if I end up getting a bath when I get home, you're to blame," said Robbie, who was thinking about the last time he had come home in a mess and had been forced into the shower for a most uncomfortable twenty minutes of scrubbing, pulling, tugging, and much cursing by his irate owners.

Some dogs love getting bathed. Robbie was not one of those dogs.

"Oh come on, you will be out in the swish of a tail," said Biffy, trotting on towards the end of the tunnel.

Robbie and Marple followed Biffy through the damp and dirty tunnel and emerged from the other end neither damp nor dirty, much to the relief of both Robbie and Marple.

The culvert ended just behind the gardens of the houses that ran along the other side of the road to Axbridge, with the small stream running along the side of Holwell Lane and down towards the reservoir.

"We could go and see what's happening at the boatyard down at the Axbridge end of the reservoir," suggested Biffy.

"OK," replied the other two, almost in unison.

So Biffy, Robbie, and Marple trotted off down the lane towards a small wood by the side of the reservoir. Once past the wood, they turned right and followed the track towards the boatyard.

"I've never been down here," said Marple. "Is the mousing good?"

"Oh, quite good, especially under the yacht club building, though I haven't been down here for a while," answered Biffy.

"Sounds like far too much exercise!" commented Robbie.

"Well you have to keep up your skills. You never know when you are going to need them in an emergency," said Biffy.

"That would be a mouse emergency, would it?" said Robbie with a snort.

Biffy stopped and turned round. He said, "Never underestimate your enemy. It's always the small, furry rodent that takes you by surprise."

Robbie looked Biffy in the eye and said, "Come on, it's not as if they're going to try and take over the world or steal all the cheese or something."

"That's exactly what they want you to think. Why do you think elephants are afraid of them?" said Biffy, and he turned round again and continued walking.

"They are a lot more dangerous than they look, you know," said Marple, passing Robbie and following Biffy.

Robbie just shook his head and said, "Cats!" then followed his friends.

As the cats and dog approached the boatyard, Biffy said, "Right, Marple, you take the left and I'll take the right so that we can check on who's been around recently."

Robbie sat on his haunches and said, "Now what are you two up to?"

Biffy turned to his doggy friend and said, "You stay here. We're just going round for a sniff to find out which cats have been around and to get a general sense of the place!"

"Suits me," said Robbie, settling down for a bit of a stretch and perhaps a sleep in the sun.

Biffy and Marple started to circle the yacht club building in opposite directions, carefully sniffing everything within reach of their noses and scent marking where appropriate.

CHAPTER 8

A Sudden Change of Plan

While Biffy and Marple checked out the yacht club, the Martian mice were still studying the lay of the land in and around the village, looking for a good landing site.

"Sir!" piped up the communications officer. "The computer has pinpointed the exact location of that broadcast. I am displaying it on the main viewing screen now."

Ensign Loudsqueak pressed a few buttons. The general raised his eyebrows ever higher with every squeak.

A small flashing red dot appeared near the bottom left-hand corner of a large, almost square area of grass near the southern edge of the village. "That's it! That's our target!" said the general excitedly. "Now where can we land?"

"We will have to be careful landing at night," said the pilot.

The general paused for a few seconds, and a strange look developed on his face as if he had just eaten something but could not decide whether he liked it or not.

"Right, I have changed our plans due to the new information we have just received about all the cheese down there. We're not going to wait until dark. We're going in now!"

Lieutenant Fondue thought that the general looked quite mad but knew better than to argue when he was in this kind of mood.

Looking closely at the scene on the viewing screen, Lieutenant Fondue said, "Sir, you see that small settlement just to the south of the target area?"

"Yes, what of it?" said the general, irritated at being woken out of his reverie.

"Well, about 700 metres to the east is a small field almost completely surrounded by trees. We could land there."

The general went to the squeakascope screen and studied the area in question.

"Yes, then we could use the hover scooters to get to that strange bit of land just to the east of the target."

"You mean the one with grass and lots of small thin stones sticking out of the ground in a strange kind of order?" asked the lieutenant.

"Yes. Though it does look rather strange, we will need to be careful when we're moving about down there, but no pussyfooting. I want this job to go quickly and by the numbers!" said the general.

"We should be able to go in on foot from there," commented Lieutenant Fondue.

If the mice had known that this strange area of grass with the thin stones was an old churchyard, full of dead humans, they may have changed their plans.

"We need to get back to the fleet," said the general breathlessly. "Retract the squeakascope and set course back to rendezvous with the other ships!"

"Yes, sir," chorused the crew, who quickly rushed to their posts and started manipulating their various controls.

Soon, the *Zulupapalulu* was zipping along just above the lunar surface back towards the dark side of the moon.

"Send a signal to the fleet: All commanders to meet in the flagship as soon as we arrive!" ordered the general.

"Yes, General!" replied Ensign Loudsqueak.

CHAPTER 9

A Surprise Flying Lesson

Meanwhile, back on Earth, Robbie was having a delightful dream in which his owners had won the lottery and were showering him with the most delicious meaty snacks and treats. He was just about to sink his teeth into the biggest beefy bone you ever did see when he was rudely shaken awake. "Hey, sleepyhead, wake up!" said Biffy, roughly shaking Robbie's head with his front paws.

"Wahhh, wahhh, what is it?" said Robbie drowsily, waking up and finding his front wet with drool.

"You were whining and growling and slobbering all over yourself," said Marple.

"Can't take you anywhere," said Biffy, with a disgusted look on his face. "Clean yourself up, you mucky pup!"

"You know, I was having the loveliest dream about bones and ... well, you know," said Robbie dreamily.

"Yes, well anyway, there is nothing much of interest down here, and it must be nearly lunchtime," said Biffy.

"Oh, please don't mention food," said Robbie with a disappointed and faraway look on his face.

"I don't fancy going all the way home just yet, even for lunch," said Marple.

"Well, there's that snack bar that usually sits on Sharpham Road, you know, down at the south end of the reservoir, just past the rugby ground," said Biffy.

"That's right," said Robbie, looking more hopeful. "The customers are usually quite friendly, and you can normally get quite a good feed down there."

"OK, let's try the snack bar then. The walk should sharpen our appetites," said Marple.

So Biffy, Marple, and Robbie trotted off back southwards towards the other end of the reservoir, where they hoped there would be some friendly snack bar customers with some spare food. As they walked, they were discussing the weather.

"It's getting quite breezy," said Marple.

"Yes, great kite flying weather," said Biffy.

Suddenly, something caught their attention. Out over the reservoir, they stopped and stared at the thing that was bobbing about just above the surface and making its way towards them.

"Is that a bird?" asked Marple.

"If it is, then it's drunk," said Biffy.

Robbie started panting and wagging his tail.

"Hey! Cool it, Robbie," said Marple.

"It's a kite. Some kid must have lost control of it, and it's blown over here," said Biffy.

The wind got a bit stronger and the kite flew straight towards them, picking up some height. It was quite large and bright blue, with a long tail of red and blue ribbons trailing out behind it in the stiff breeze. As it passed over their heads, it bobbed down and skirted the ground. Robbie was off like a flash.

"Hey, Robbie!" shouted Biffy.

But Robbie had snapped into automatic pilot mode and saw only something to chase. Barking like mad, he caught hold of the kite tail just as a strong gust of wind blew the kite high into the air, taking Robbie with it.

Biffy and Marple watched in stunned amazement as the kite swirled round and back out over the water, carrying the now whining Robbie with it. Another sudden change in direction brought kite and dog back towards the shore again.

As it passed overhead again, Biffy shouted up, "Let go of the tail, you idiot!"

"Aaaaarrrrg!"

Following Biffy's advice, Robbie let go and came hurtling towards the ground but luckily found something soft to land on.

"Oumff!" said Biffy as he was crushed to the ground by about 9 kilograms of flying dog.

"Gee thanks, Biffy, you saved my neck there," said Robbie.

"OK! Now get off, you big clumsy oaf!" said Biffy in a strained voice.

"Sorry, mate," said Robbie, getting off of the quite flattened Biffy.

Marple came up to Robbie and said, "You know that habit of thinking that you are out for a walk with your owners is going to get you into trouble one day, mate."

"Sorry, guys, I just forget and lose control. It's all that conditioning and training that we dogs get," said Robbie apologetically.

"Just try and keep a lid on it," said Biffy.

"OK, sorry," said Robbie, giving his tail a little wag.

"Good boy," said Marple, winking.

Biffy gave Marple a searching look and said, "Right, let's try and get to lunch without any more adventures. I am looking forward to a nice quiet and relaxing afternoon."

"What could possibly happen now? The chances of something else happening must be astronomical," said Marple.

He was, for a change, quite right – about it being astronomical, that is!

Chapter 10

The General's New Plan

As Biffy and his mates headed south towards the snack bar and a free lunch (or so they hoped), the *Zulupapalulu* was returning to the dark side of the moon where the other five ships were waiting. Once the flagship arrived, the general called a staff meeting.

The captains of the other ships came over to the flagship on space scooters: small, one-mouse rocket craft that looked like a shopping trolley stuck on top of a gas cylinder.

Once all five captains were aboard, everyone crowded into the ship's bridge. "There's no room to swing a cockroach in here," whispered the communications officer to Lieutenant Fondue, who just managed to stifle a giggle.

"Lower the main display screen, Loudsqueak, and bring up the pictures of the landing site."

The display screen clicked into place, and a video image of the landing site appeared. The red dot was still blinking away to show where the radio signal had come from. It was in the middle of a small huddle of trucks and caravans that were parked behind a collection of large, square, and rectangular tents and marquees.

The general took up his baton and, using it as a pointer, started to explain the key points on the photograph.

"This, gentlemice, is the main arena," he said, pointing to the tents. "The four biggest tents seem to be where the cheese is being exhibited." Next he pointed the baton at the winking red light. "These trucks are where the radio signal we intercepted is coming from. The BBC people must be there." Next he pointed to an area away to the right of the image. "This small field surrounded by trees is where are going to land the fleet."

The other captains nodded in agreement and murmured their approval.

"Once landed," he continued, "we will hightail it on the hover scooters to this location here." He pointed to the old churchyard.

"Then we hide the scooters and go in on foot to get the cheese."

Before he could stop himself, Lieutenant Fondue interrupted the general. "How?" he said, and turned red on hearing himself.

"How what?" asked the general, in an exasperated voice.

"Well, err," stuttered the lieutenant, suddenly aware that everyone on the bridge was looking at him.

"Out with it, mouse!" roared the general.

"Well, how do we get all that cheese back to the scooters if we are on foot?"

Now everyone turned to look at the general. It was a bit like watching a tennis match at Wimbledon.

It was the general's turn to go red and look flustered. However, he recovered quickly enough to avoid letting the captains suspect that he had been making up these plans as he went along.

The general noisily cleared his throat and said, "I wondered how long it would take you to spot that, Lieutenant. Well done!" But he was thinking, *I'll get you later for that, Fondue!*

"We will, of course, be taking one scooter per group fitted with side-saddle sacks to carry the cheese." He was just fixing the lieutenant with a nasty stare when another question came from the lieutenant's lips. His brain was now sitting back and enjoying the show his mouth was making.

"Will the cheese not be guarded, sir?"

All heads now turned back to the lieutenant. The general was really annoyed now with the way his splendidly simple plan had suddenly become complicated, due in part to Fondue and his clever Dick questions, but in reality mostly due to the general being an idiot.

Going slightly purple, the general turned to the captains and said waspishly, "Of course it will be guarded. That's why we have Captain Cheesestick and his diversionary tactics."

All heads, especially Captain Cheesestick, turned to look at the general again.

Lieutenant Fondue looked up in surprise as the general, looking directly at him, said, "Well, Lieutenant, any more questions?"

All eyes on Fondue again.

It was the lieutenant's turn to be annoyed now, so he said (without really thinking), "I'm sure the general will share these diversionary tactics with the rest of us."

You could almost hear the swish as all heads turned to watch the general again.

The general's eyebrows were almost touching the ceiling. He looked furious and was going quite mad.

Really winging it now, the general said, "Captain Cheesestick will go in ahead of the main raiding party with

a small diversionary squad and blow up the radio trucks."
The general looked rather pleased at his new idea and started
to compose himself again. He would sort out Fondue once
this was all over. He then said, "This will cause an alarm,
and the tents will be cleared, giving us the chance to get in
and among all the confusion grab the cheese!"

There was a brief pause before the general said, "Now
unless there are any more questions ..."

All eyes were on Fondue, who said nothing but thought,
This is going to go horribly wrong, which, strangely, seemed to
cheer him up a bit.

"OK!" All eyes back on the general. "Return to your
ships, and on my signal follow me to Earth and the landing
site!"

"Aye, aye!" said the captains, saluting as one. They left
to go back to their ships.

As soon as they were back on board their ships, the other
captains ordered the saddlebags to be brought out of stores
and fitted to the hover scooters. Once this was done, they
signalled the flagship that they were all ready to go.

"OK, Stilton, full speed ahead!"

Space Pilot Stilton pressed several buttons and switches
on his panel, and the ship's rocket motors roared into life.

Once the flagship's own special scooter was fitted with
its saddlebags, the general turned to the communications
officer and ordered, "Loudsqueak, give the rest of the fleet
the signal to start!"

"Yes, sir!" replied Loudsqueak.

The pilot pulled several sliding controls down to their
maximum, and the *Zulupapalulu* roared off into space,
followed quickly by the rest of the invasion fleet, towards
an unsuspecting earth.

Chapter 11

Siesta Time

Meanwhile, back on Earth, Biffy, Robbie, and Marple had not been disappointed by the friendliness of the snack bar's customers or their generosity. The snack bar owner did not mind having the odd dog or cat about. He said it kept the rats down.

"Oh boy, I'm stuffed," said Robbie yawing and licking his chops.

"Yes, I could do with a nice after-lunch nap – you know, like they do in the more civilised parts of mainland Europe. *Siesta*, that's what they call it. How about you, Marple?" asked Biffy.

"Sounds great. Let's go round to the far south end of the reservoir where those small, tree-surrounded fields are and lie up for a bit."

"OK, let's go. Shouldn't be disturbed by anything too earth- shattering this afternoon, what do you think?" said Biffy.

"Well I, for one, have had quite enough excitement for one day, thank you very much," replied Robbie.

"Yeah, nothing much happens round here," agreed Marple, "providing you don't go running off after runaway kites," he added as an afterthought and gave Robbie a playful poke in the ribs.

"Look, what's the chance of that happening again?" laughed Robbie.

"As I said earlier, probably astronomical," said Marple.

"Yes, well, the sooner we get there, the sooner I can have a nice long sleep," said Biffy.

So the three friends trotted off to have a nice long rest at the south end of the reservoir, content to spend the rest of the day holed up in a lovely quiet spot, totally unaware that soon it would become (contrary to expectations) the centre of some astronomical – or we should say *astronautical* events.

CHAPTER 12

An Emergency Landing

As Biffy and his friends were heading for a nice quiet after-lunch sleep, the Martian fleet were zooming at full speed through the atmosphere and were soon skimming its upper reaches. It took a few orbits to gradually lower their speed before they started the main descent towards the southwest of England and the village of Cheddar. This manoeuvre is called *aerobraking* by space engineers.

You may well be thinking: Why did no one notice six small rockets zooming about in the air? Surely someone at Air Traffic Control or Strategic Air Defence Command would notice them. By a strange coincidence, the moon dust that the Martian ships were coated in to hide the ships on the moon also deflected and confused ground-based radar. On radar, it looked like a flock of geese or something and was ignored.

In the control bridge of the *Zulupapalulu*, everything was going exactly to plan.

"How long until we reach the landing site, Stilton?" asked the general.

"About thirty minutes, sir," replied the busy pilot.

"Fondue, are all the hover scooters that we are going to take into the cheese tents now fitted with their side-saddle packs?" asked the general, turning to his second in command.

"Yes, sir, each ship has one scooter fully fitted to take as much cheese as we can handle, and another three scooters each for the mice coming on the raid, which leaves two mice behind on each ship."

The general made a quick calculation. "So with myself and you, Fondue, that gives us eighteen mice for the raid and four on the diversion?"

"Yes, sir," replied Fondue.

"Good, looks like nothing can go wrong," said the general cheerfully.

Suddenly, a loud klaxon went off, and a red light started to flash on the pilot's control panel.

"Sir, the rocket motors are overheating. We need to refill the coolant tank. Any old water will do, but we must do it soon, or we will blow up!"

The general thought to himself, I knew we shouldn't have got the ships from that scoundrel of a second hand *spaceship dealer, Honest Edam.* The general looked up at the display screen and said, "There is a large, round lake just to the west of the village. If we can make it to there, we can touch down and fill our tanks there."

"Won't that give away our surprise if we are seen going down to the lake so close to the village?" asked Fondue, worried.

"Can't help that now!" said the anxious general as he rushed over to the pilot's control console.

"Look there," said the general, pointing to the south end of the reservoir on the pilot's viewing screen. The pilot's control console had a small video screen that had the view ahead and below on a split screen.

"There are several small tree-enclosed fields at the south end. We can land there and hide in the trees."

"It's a bit far from the water's edge to pump," said Fondue, turning to the pilot. "How much hose do we have on board?" he asked the pilot.

"About 100 metres, sir," replied Pilot Stilton.

"That should be enough," said the general. "It looks like about 70 metres to the edge of the lake. OK, Stilton, take us down and land as near to the trees by the water's edge as you can!"

"Yes, sir!" replied the pilot, who started to steer the ship towards the reservoir. The whole crew held their breath as they desperately tried to get to the source of water to cool the engines before they blew up.

General Squeakcheesy turned to the communications console and said, "Ensign Loudsqueak."

"Yes, sir?"

"Inform the other ships that we have to make an emergency detour via the lake, but they are to continue and to land as planned at the landing site to the east of the village."

"Yes, sir."

"Tell them to wait there until we can join them. Better tell them to remain in their ships as well, but they are to keep a lookout in case we've been spotted," finished the general.

"Yes, sir," replied Loudsqueak, who started clicking switches on his panel so that he could relay the general's orders to the rest of the fleet.

CHAPTER 13

Is It a Bird? Is It a Plane?

Unaware that they were about to be invaded, Biffy, Marple, and Robbie had reached the southern end of the reservoir and were looking for a nice spot to sleep away a few lazy afternoon hours.

"Here we are," said Biffy. "We can rest up under those trees that line the lane there."

"Looks good to me," said Robbie. "Bit of sun, bit of shade, and nice and peaceful."

"Well, nothing is going to disturb me for a few hours," said Marple.

Of course all three of them were dead wrong.

Biffy had curled himself up into a ball, wrapping his tail around his body. Marple was just getting comfortable when Robbie exclaimed, "What's that?"

"What's what?" asked Biffy, without getting up.

"There's something in the air just above the far end of the reservoir, and its heading this way," replied Robbie.

"Not another kite?" said Marple, getting up and smiling at Robbie.

"Probably a bird, a swan or something," said Biffy with his eyes still closed.

"Well, it's travelling awfully fast for a swan, mate," said Robbie.

Reluctantly, Biffy opened his eyes and got up for a look and had just started to comment. "Could be a ..."

Rrrrrrrroooarweeeeeeeeeeeeeeee!

Biffy never finished his sentence because all three of them dived for cover in the grass just as the thing that Biffy had thought was probably a swan came roaring overhead with a mighty, wailing scream, something like a lion roaring but with a loud whistling kettle in the background.

A few moments later, the terrible sound died away, and Biffy looked up and opened one eye. "Holy mackerel! That was no swan!"

"You don't say," said Robbie, sarcastically.

"I think it came down behind those trees just the other side of the lane," said Marple, getting up out of the grass.

"Well, it hasn't crashed, or we would have heard it hit the ground. Must have landed," said Biffy, standing up with his tail all bushed up.

"Let's go and have a peep," said Marple, slowly edging towards the lane that ran round the bottom of the reservoir between lines of trees.

"Are you crazy?" whispered Robbie nervously.

"I thought you were looking for glory and trumpets and really wild times," said Biffy, remembering the conversation from earlier that morning.

"Yeah, well that didn't include crazy screaming rocket-propelled swans!" answered still-trembling Robbie.

CHAPTER 14

A Dastardly Plan Revealed

Meanwhile, on board the Martian spaceship, Space Pilot Stilton was hurriedly shutting down the now red-hot, and about-to-explode rocket motors. "Phew, just made it. Another couple of minutes and there would have been mouse toast all over the countryside!" he said.

"Shut up, Stilton and start preparing the water pumps," barked General Squeakcheesy, greatly relieved.

"We will have to wait about thirty minutes until everything has cooled down a bit. We may have avoided becoming toast, but we can still end up poached," said Stilton.

"OK, where's Loudsqueak?"

The communications officer got up from where he had been hiding under his console during the emergency landing. "Here, sir!" he said, dusting himself off.

"Raise the periscope. I want to have a look round. Hopefully we didn't bring any unwanted attention to ourselves."

As Loudsqueak operated the controls to deploy the periscope, the main viewing screen slid down from the ceiling again and flickered to life.

Lieutenant Fondue said, "The humans on earth do seem to be rather unobservant, though that flock of geese certainly had a big surprise."

"Well, looks like we got away with it," said the general, who was scanning an image on the viewing screen that showed the spacecraft's immediate surroundings.

"Yep, there's nothing out there that's intelligent enough to have observed us and give us any trouble."

Of course the mice were dead wrong, especially about the trouble.

"OK, let's suit up and get that water tank filled as quickly as possible. You know, I feel lucky today!" said the general, cheerfully. He was dead wrong about that, too.

***

Meanwhile, Biffy was rallying his troops. "Come on," he said, nodding in the direction of the landing site. "We have to see what's going on."

So they slowly crept up onto the lane and across to where some shrubs provided excellent cover from where they could look into the area behind the trees without being observed themselves.

Nothing could have prepared them for the scene in front of them. The grass was still burning in places from the rocket's touchdown blast. A large amount of steam was coming from the bottom of the spaceship, which was sitting on its four tail fins, pointing up at the sky. It looked like one of those Second World War German V2 rockets, only smaller. In fact, the rocket's height was just less than 4 meters high, which is roughly the same as the length of the average family car, and it was a little wider as at its widest point than an old-fashioned metal dustbin, say about 60 centimetres. So if you can imagine four dustbins piled on top of each other with a pointed nose cone on top, sitting on four fins at the bottom, then that's quite close. There were also several portholes near the nose cone.

A couple of small creatures wearing silver suits and round helmets with long, pointed faceplates were busily scurrying around the tail fins. They were carrying what looked like a long hose that came from the bottom of the ship and were heading down towards the water's edge with it.

Meanwhile, another couple of the creatures were standing quite close to where Biffy was hiding and seemed to be in command as they were dressed differently from the others.

The one that seemed to be in charge had gold cuffs and shoulder patches. It was currently conversing with one bearing silver insignia.

"Everything seems to be in order, General," said the one with silver patches.

Biffy sat amazed, not just at the scene in front of him, but also by the fact that these creatures were speaking English. Granted, it was a bit high-pitched and squeaky, but it was English nevertheless. It may seem a rather extraordinary coincidence that the Martians spoke English, but was in fact an amazing example of parallel evolution.

Marple and Robbie, sitting either side of Biffy, also sat watching the scene in amazement.

"What are they?" asked Marple.

"Not sure. They're quite small, seem to have pointed faces, and yes – look – long, hairless tails. That definitely reminds me of something!"

The space-suited creature with the silver patches said to his compatriot, "Stilton says the air is OK, sir. We can take our helmets off." He reached up and unclasped his helmet and took a large breath of air before taking it off. "Smells OK, General." Then he removed the helmet.

Biffy gave out a long gasp. "Holy Toledo, they're mice!"

"They seem to be a bit big for mice. Are you sure they're not rats?" asked Marple.

Biffy gave the air a long, careful sniff. "Yep, definitely mice. Big mice, I grant you, but still mice."

"Just one thing, though," said Robbie. "Are they supposed to be that colour?"

"OK, they're green, but they're still mice," answered Biffy.

General Squeakcheesy turned to Lieutenant Fondue and said, "How long till the water tanks are full and we can join the rest of the fleet at the main landing site?"

"About fifteen minutes, sir. Why?"

"Not sure, I keep getting a strange feeling that we are being watched," said the general, looking about suspiciously.

"Well the cat detector has registered nothing, so I would not worry too much. It's probably something in the air," said the lieutenant, who was sniffing and trying to detect anything strange.

Unbeknown to the lieutenant, the cat detector had been disconnected by the ship's last owner because it made a horribly irritating noise when operating, something like an owl with hiccups.

"OK, Lieutenant, once we are back with the rest of the fleet at the main landing site, we will unload the hover scooters and head straight for the cheese festival." The general liked to go over his plans several times like this, more to convince himself that they would work than for any other reason.

"Yes, sir!" added the lieutenant. "Then Captain Cheesecake will start his diversion by blowing up the radio truck."

"Right. Once everyone has evacuated the main tents, we charge in and steal all their cheese, zip back to the ships, and then it's home to Mars for a big cheesy supper."

The Martian general was totally unaware that he had just divulged their entire plan to Biffy and his friends.

CHAPTER 15

A Skateboard, a Little Girl, and a Big Problem

Biffy put one paw to his lips to indicate that silence was needed and nodded back to the lane away from the Martians and their dastardly plans.

Once safely out of sight and earshot, Biffy turned to his friends and said, "We have to stop them. If they get away with stealing all that cheese, who knows what they may try next? Nip it in the bud, that's what I say!"

Robbie, who had said nothing until now, said, "It's easier to shout Stop! than to do it."

Biffy looked him in the eyes and replied, "What's that famous saying again? All that is needed for evil to triumph is for one good cat to do nothing!" Biffy paused slightly before continuing: "Well, I'm going to do something!"

"But we don't even know where this cheese thingy is taking place," argued Robbie.

Biffy thought for a minute and then said, "Hey, there's that caravan site just behind the tennis club – you know, just at the end of the lane here near to where Sharpham Road starts. There should be a notice board there telling visitors about what's going on in the village."

"Great idea, Biffy. There should be a notice or poster about something this important up there," agreed Marple.

"OK, let's get up there quickly! Looks like those mice are ready to set off again," said Robbie, looking back towards where the spaceship lay hidden behind the trees.

Just then, there was a roar and a blast of heat as the rocket took off into the sky and then dipped towards the south of the village.

"OK, quick, let's get to the tennis club!" said Biffy, taking off at a run back along Middle Moor Lane towards the village with the other two following as quickly as they could.

After what seemed like ages, they arrived panting at the entrance to the caravan site, and sure enough, there was a large notice board held up by two wooden posts.

"Robbie, come here, I need a bit more height to see what's up here!" commanded Biffy.

"What do you think I am, a blooming footstool?" replied Robbie, not at all pleased about his new role in life.

"Stop complaining. We have a world to save. Now stand about here!" said Biffy, indicating a point just in front of the middle of the notice board.

Robbie came over and stood in the appointed position. "The things I do for you guys," he said.

Ignoring Robbie's complaints and mumblings, Biffy jumped up onto the dog's back.

"Whoa, you need to lose some weight, you big, fat ..." But at that moment, Robbie was silenced. In the process of finding a more comfortable position, one of Biffy's paws had lodged itself in the dog's mouth while the other was wedged in his right ear.

"Ouch, votch if," spluttered Robbie.

"Oh keep still, will you. I'm trying to read this notice," replied Biffy.

"Vell huffy up. Uf I vanted to oo vis kind of shing I vould huf oined the fircus," spluttered Robbie.

Biffy jumped down, and Robbie said, now that his mouth was not filled with cat, "That was not funny!"

Biffy ignored him and said, "It's at that school down by St Andrews. They're having it in the playing fields."

"Yes, I remember the place – the Rings of Essex or something," said Marple.

"Kings of Wessex, you twit," said Robbie stretching his now rather painful back.

"Whatever it's called, we need to get there fast!" cried Biffy.

"OK, what's the quickest way to get there?" asked Robbie.

Marple, who thought he knew the village as much as anyone, said, "Well, at the end of this road we can turn down Lower New Road, then turn and go along Wedmore Road until it meets Station Road. The school is just south of there."

"The only problem with that is that Wedmore Road goes uphill. If we take that lane from the end of Sharpham Road, the one that runs behind those houses in Fourways Crescent, it eventually leads to Wedmore Road, and that's still quite near to the school and it's downhill all the way."

"What difference does it make whether it's going uphill or downhill?" asked Robbie.

"Because I have just seen a way to get down to the school really quickly," said Biffy, who had been formulating a mad plan in his head for the last few minutes.

"Right, guys, here's the plan," said Biffy, with a mad and quite alarming look in his eyes.

"You see that skateboard lying by the door of that caravan?"

"Yeah," replied Robbie, who was beginning to think that trouble was not very far away.

"We are going to commandeer that skateboard."

"Whoa!" said a rather alarmed Robbie. "What do you mean 'commandeer' it?"

"We need to get down to the school fast, and this is the only way I can think of. It's downhill all the way and shouldn't be too much trouble for the three of us," said Biffy, looking at the other two as if there was no questioning his decision or the sanity of his intentions.

"The three of us on one skateboard?" questioned Marple, who then added, "Are you out of your tiny mind?"

Biffy ignored the comment and said, "Come on, it'll be fun!"

"Oh well, if it's going to be fun, I'm in!" said Marple.

Biffy looked at Robbie and said, "Robbie, go and get that skateboard and bring it here!"

"Why me?" asked the alarmed dog.

"Because that's what dogs are good at – fetching things. So go fetch!"

"Go fetch, indeed!" said Robbie as he reluctantly headed over to the caravan in question. Robbie was about halfway there when the caravan door opened and a little girl about 9 years old came out and playfully jumped down the small set of steps in front of the caravan door.

Robbie just froze where he was.

"Hello, little doggy," she said in a friendly manner. Robbie had to think quickly. Biffy and Marple hid behind the fence when they saw the door opening.

"Woof!" said Robbie, and wagged his tail.

The little girl looked at him with that questioning face that children use when thinking through something difficult but important. She cocked her head to one side and said, "Did you just say woof?"

Biffy and Marple looked on helplessly. Biffy whispered to no one in particular, "Come on, stop playing the little lost doggy and just grab that skateboard."

Robbie, suddenly realising his mistake, gave a happy little bark and wagged his tail again. The little girl said, "Hmm, I think I will take you to the police. You look lost!" and skipped right up to the incredulous dog.

Biffy knew he had to do something at once to save the situation, so while the little girl's full attention was on Robbie, quick as a flash he sprang forward, surprising both Marple and himself in the process.

"What on earth?" said Marple as Biffy sped over to the unfolding disaster.

Just as the little girl stretched down to pick Robbie up, something rubbed against her leg. Looking down, she saw a large tabby cat with an odd orange tip on the end of his tail.

"Hmm!" said the girl. "Hello, pussy cat, where did you come from?" While her attention was now on Biffy, Robbie sneaked away and hid behind the caravan.

Biffy was keeping the girl busy by rolling over onto his back and allowing her to rub his tummy.

Marple, meanwhile, was trying to get Robbie's attention by sitting on his haunches and waving madly in a very un-catlike way, mouthing the words, "Get the skateboard! Get the skateboard!"

The girl suddenly looked up from rubbing Biffy's tummy and noticed Marple trying to get Robbie's attention. She put her hands on her hips and said, "Now what is that cat doing?"

Marple suddenly became aware that he had been spotted and quickly snuck away, back behind the fence. To keep the girl's attention, Biffy started purring and rubbing up against her legs again.

To his horror and the utter amazement of the other two animals, she bent down and quickly picked Biffy up into her arms.

"Now, what are you animals up to?" said the girl, holding fast to the squirming cat. "I think I will take you into the caravan and give you some milk."

She turned and headed back towards the caravan door. Robbie suddenly decided to take desperate action. Tearing round from behind the caravan, he grabbed the skateboard in his mouth and tore off through the gates of the caravan site.

The little girl dropped Biffy in surprise and shouted, "Hey! That's my brother's!"

Biffy did not wait around to see what happened. He shot through the gate and followed Robbie, with Marple following behind at a run.

The little girl ran to the gate, but the animals had disappeared from sight in a cloud of dust.

"This must be a Wednesday," said the girl for no apparent reason and skipped off back to the caravan.

CHAPTER 16

Who Put That Hedge There?

After the three of them had run as fast as they could for several minutes, Robbie glanced round and saw that the girl was not following them. Slowing down, he said breathlessly, "It's OK, we're not being followed." So they all stopped for a moment to catch their breaths.

Dropping the skateboard and panting hard, Robbie said, "Phew! That was close!"

"Close!" said Biffy. "Why on earth did you say woof in front of that little girl? Do you want the humans to realise that we can all speak English?"

"Sorry, but things seem to be getting a bit out of hand just lately. And in case you hadn't noticed, it was my caboose that was hanging out on the line."

"It wasn't you who was outrageously manhandled just now!" said Biffy. "The nerve of it – 'pussy' indeed!" he said indignantly.

Marple observed that it had at least got them to the end of Sharpham Road. And they had the skateboard!

"OK, now what?" asked Robbie.

Biffy sat in thought for a while, then said, "Right, the top of the lane is just round that corner. Let's get there so we can get on the skateboard and get down to the cheese festival!"

"And I suppose I have to carry it?" asked Robbie.

"You suppose correctly!" answered Biffy, taking off towards the top of the lane.

Robbie picked up the skateboard in his mouth and, following Biffy, started muttering complaints that sounded a bit like "Ratten, dratten, fiddlen, stuffen, skateboarden ..." and so on.

After a few minutes walk, the three friends plus skateboard reached the top of the lane that would take them down to where Wedmore Road met Station Road.

"Right," said Biffy. "Once we get to the bottom of the lane, we can cut through the business park and into the school grounds from the back."

"OK, how are all three of us going to get on the skateboard?" asked a rather sceptical Robbie.

"I will go up front. Marple, you get on behind me, and Robbie, you can cover the rear!"

"Sounds like a one-way ticket to the vets," said Robbie resignedly. They made a strange sight, hurtling down the lane behind the houses of Fourways Crescent.

Biffy was sitting up in front like a meerkat, with Marple leaning on his shoulders. Robbie was standing on his hind legs and holding on to Marple for grim death, whimpering all the while.

"Oh stop that whimpering and get some backbone, you big wimp!" shouted Biffy, but his words were stolen away on the wind as it rushed past.

**

Strangely, those words ended up in the oddest of places. Carried by the wind over half the country, they re-appeared in a smart restaurant in Reading, where a shy young man was attempting to impress his date with what he thought was a clever and witty anecdote that would win her heart. Of course he was dead wrong.

Suddenly from nowhere, the words "Oh, stop that whimpering and get some backbone, you big wimp!" came out of his mouth. By the time he had wiped the wine out of his eyes, the girl had gone, but the bill hadn't.

**

Meanwhile, back in Cheddar, Mrs Wellforgotten was staring out of the kitchen window of No. 11 Fourways Crescent. The window looked out over her back garden, where she liked to watch the garden birds flutter about the many feeding boxes that her children had put up. She was having a little break from peeling the potatoes for dinner. She was thinking that nothing unusual ever happened around there. Of course she was dead wrong.

She was admiring the azaleas down by the low stone wall that ran along the bottom of her garden, and had begun dreamily peeling the potatoes again when suddenly Biffy, Robbie, and Marple went hurtling by on the skateboard down the lane behind the houses. Mrs Wellforgotten stopped in mid-peel and blinked several times. "I need more sleep," she said to herself, and dutifully went back to work on her King Edward.

As the unlikely threesome sped down towards the bottom of the lane at great speed, Biffy realised that a sharp bend to the right was coming up very fast. "Corner coming up!" he shouted, trying not to sound too panicky.

"Does anyone know how to steer this thing?" yelled Marple.

After a few seconds of quick thinking, during which the corner came whooshing towards them, Biffy breathlessly shouted, "OK, when I say lean, everyone lean to the right!"

"*Lean!*" screamed Biffy.

All three leaned over as far as they could without falling off. The skateboard's left-hand side lifted off the ground, and the board spun round to the right at a whirlwind speed. As the skateboard's wheels touched back down again and the board sped on in the new direction, they all breathed again.

Their relief was to be short-lived, though, as they realised that another bend, this time to the left, was almost upon them.

"*Lean!*" screamed Biffy.

This time all three leaned quickly to the left, and again the skateboard spun round the corner then righted itself safely.

"Well, that worked!" shouted Biffy against the tearing wind that was whipping away his words as the skateboard rocketed down the lane.

"OK, we now know how to steer this thing," shouted Robbie, "but how do we stop it?"

Suddenly, Biffy realised that they had run out of time for another turn. In the few seconds that remained, he shouted, "I think this hedge will help. *Arrrggghh!*"

Biffy, the skateboard, and the others crashed right into a large, thick hedge. The skateboard, minus occupants and two wheels, shot out the other side and came to a halt a few metres further on.

After a few seconds of shocked silence, there was a muffled confusion of moaning and cursing before Biffy said, "Well, that wasn't too bad. I seem to have had a rather soft landing."

"That's because you're sitting on my head, you big oaf!" said Robbie, annoyed.

"Won't have done any damage then," said Biffy in a slightly raised voice.

"Now guys, let's not start quarrelling," said a disembodied voice from somewhere nearby.

"Where are you?" asked Biffy, looking around and noticing Marple's absence for the first time.

"I'm up here."

Biffy, who had removed himself from Robbie's head and dropped down to the space at the bottom of the hedge, looked up to where Marple sat uncomfortably in a large bird's-nest.

"You make a strange cuckoo," said Biffy.

"What are you doing up there?" asked Robbie.

"Well, I thought I would try roosting," replied Marple, sarcastically.

The other two were directly below the nest when Marple said "Hey, guys, I'm not sure how stable this thing is. *Arrgghh!*"

Down came Marple, nest and all, right on top of poor Robbie.

"Hoi, I wish you guys would stop landing on me!" complained Robbie, rubbing his head."

"Sorry, mate," said Marple, pulling bits of hedge and the occasional feather from his fur.

All three of them now sat in the space beneath the hedge.

"Where are we, anyway?" asked Robbie.

Biffy got up and peered through the other side of the hedge.

"We appear to be near the business park, which means that the school and the cheese festival are not far away."

In fact Biffy, Marple, and Robbie could actually hear the distant but unmistakable sounds that one usually associates with large public events, the collective murmur of crowds of people laughing and talking, generators, and music.

CHAPTER 17

The Explosive Backpack

Meanwhile, the Martian mice were putting together the final preparations for the raid on the cheese festival. The *Zulupapalulu* had at last made it safely to the planned landing site without any further disasters while Biffy and his friends were busy trying to outwit that 9-year-old girl and steal the skateboard.

At this point you may be wondering why someone in Cheddar hadn't noticed several rockets buzzing about the sky, especially when the *Zulupapalulu* went screaming over the reservoir during its emergency landing. It so happens that the RAF liked to use Cheddar Gorge as a bomb run practice spot and regularly carried out low-flying practice flights over Cheddar. The local inhabitants were so used to the noise of screaming jets that a few rockets buzzing around arose no undue attention whatsoever.

The mice had unloaded all the hover scooters that they were to use to get to the target area. They looked a bit like a cross between a tiny kid's scooter and a narrow steam iron with motorbike-like handlebars at the front. When all the scooters were assembled, it looked like a 1960s mod rally.

There were the five special scooters with saddlebags that would carry the cheese. Off to one side were the four scooters that would go on ahead and create the diversion led by Captain Cheesecake. That left fifteen scooters that were the main raiding party.

Now that the air had been verified as safe, the mice had shed their space suits and were wearing dark camouflage fatigues and what looked like dark green American football helmets. The general was giving a last briefing to the diversion squad, who were to set off ten minutes before the main raiding party. "OK, Cheesecake, you know what you have to do!"

"Yes, sir. We get to the place with all the stones, leave the scooters, and go in on foot. Once we locate the radio truck, we blow it up."

"Yes, hug the tree and hedge lines, and keep low for as long as possible until you hit the outskirts of the village. We need to keep the element of surprise," said the general.

"Understood, sir," replied Cheesecake.

"Have you have got the explosives?" asked the general.

"Yes, sir. Private Thinsqueak has them in his backpack."

A very nervous-looking mouse wearing a backpack sat on his scooter in a very unnaturally and rigid position.

"Is he all right?" asked the general. "He looks a bit nervous."

"Wouldn't you be?" replied Cheesecake. "He is carrying enough goudamite to blow up a house."

"Steady there, son," said the general in what he hoped was a fatherly manner. "Just think about all that cheese." The general then gave the poor mouse an encouraging slap on the back.

The entire invasion force, except for the general, Captain Cheesecake, and the unfortunate Thinsqueak, threw themselves onto the ground and covered their ears with their paws, waiting for the resulting explosion.

When the explosion failed to materialise, the relieved mice got up and started dusting themselves off.

The nervous mouse with the explosive backpack was looking paler than ever. He just blinked a few times and sat frozen to the saddle of his scooter. He was trying not to move a single muscle unless he had to.

A short time earlier, Captain Cheesecake had asked for a volunteer from his squad to carry the bomb. When asked to step one pace forward, Thinsqueak's comrades quickly all took one step backward, leaving him out in front.

Captain Cheesecake mounted his scooter and signalled his mice to start up. All four scooters rose silently and hovered about 25 centimetres above the ground.

The general drew back and spoke into his wrist communicator, which looked a bit like a large wristwatch. "OK, Cheesecake, you have a 20-minute lead to set up and activate the diversion. Off you go." Captain Cheesecake saluted, and the four hover scooters of the diversionary squad moved off silently in the direction of the churchyard.

The general gave the order for the rest of the raiding party to mount up.

"OK, mice," he said into his wrist, "in twenty minutes you will follow me in single file in your groups."

The general had organised his cheese snatch squads by their original rocket assignments. He continued, "We will hug the tree and hedge lines, keeping as low as possible until we hit the edge of the village."

After the twenty minutes were up, General Squeakcheesy started his scooter and gave the order to advance.

One by one, the Martian hover scooters rose up and glided silently after the general, following him in single file. It made quite a sight: twenty mice sitting on floating steam irons.

CHAPTER 18

The Emergency

Meanwhile, not that far away, Biffy stuck his head back inside the hedge and turned to his fellow adventurers. He said, "OK, we need to get down to Wedmore road. It's just past this hedge a bit."

"How far is a bit?" asked Robbie, who was still rubbing his head.

"Should only take us about three or four minutes if we run. The skateboard's a goner," replied Biffy.

"OK, let's get going," said Marple.

"Wait up," said Biffy. "Let's plan this properly." And he sat down and thought for a few moments, after which he said, "Right, once we get to the road, we have to cross it and then go down by the side of the leisure centre and into the school sports grounds."

"Then what?" asked Robbie.

"We will decide that when we get there," said Biffy, getting up and slipping out of the hedge into the afternoon sun on the other side.

As soon as the other two had followed Biffy out of the hedge, they took off at a fast trot. As Biffy had thought, it only took about four minutes to reach Wedmore Road. When they all got safely across, Biffy, Marple, and Robbie took off again towards the leisure centre.

As they drew nearer, the crowd noises got louder, and they knew that they were nearly at the festival.

"OK, slow down. We don't want any unwanted attention," said Biffy.

"Yeah, let's avoid any small girls with skateboards," said Robbie sarcastically.

"You weren't the one she was squashing in her arms," said Biffy.

"Yeah, well 'Go fetch the skateboard!' That was your great idea," growled Robbie.

"Guys, can you continue this some other time? We're here!" interrupted Marple.

Our three would-be heroes were standing near the corner of the leisure centre. Looking out onto the sports ground, they could see the large square of grass that normally consisted of a cricket pitch, a running track, and various other sports pitches. It was currently covered by about a dozen tents and marquees of various shapes and sizes. There were also lots of stalls, selling everything from cardboard gliders to hot dogs.

"OK, what do we do now?" asked Robbie.

"We need to find those mice. They must have landed somewhere to the southeast, where there are lots of small fields surrounded by trees for cover," answered Biffy.

"Well, we could skirt round to the west and down along that line of trees that separate the playing fields from that waste ground just to the west of the industrial estate," suggested Marple.

"Yes, then we can follow that small river that runs along the bottom. Most of the big tents seem to be down at this end anyway," said Biffy.

"Right, let's get going!" said Robbie.

So Biffy, Robbie, and Marple went off to skirt round the western edge of the festival and approach from the south end, where most of the big tents and marquees were. They were soon trotting along the southern edge of the sports ground, heading back east, and keeping under the cover of a short hedge that had the occasional tree growing out of it.

At this point both our friends here and the Martian diversionary squad were heading straight for each other, and would have spotted each other had they not been on opposite sides of the hedge.

Robbie suddenly stopped and said, "Sorry guys, I have to go."

Biffy stopped and turned round to face Robbie.

"What do you mean, you have to go? Go where, for Pete's sake?" he asked exasperatedly.

"You know – call of nature," whispered Robbie slightly embarrassed.

"And you had to wait until now?" added Marple.

"Hey, when you have to go, you have to go," replied Robbie defensively.

"OK, hurry up. We'll wait here for you," said Biffy.

So Robbie slunk off to do his business and returned a minute or so later.

"All fine now," he said looking relieved.

"Oh good," said Biffy. "Is it OK if we continue trying to save the world now?" he added, giving Robbie a steely stare. Robbie grinned slyly and wagged his tail a bit.

Of course by this time the mice's diversionary squad had turned round and were about to activate their plan.

"OK, let's continue, shall we? Since we couldn't see anything up the top end that looked like this BBC broadcast truck, it must be down here at the southern end," said Biffy.

"Yes, that's where their diversionary attack is going to take place," Marple added.

"We could try and stop them there," proposed Robbie.

"No, we need to find the main landing site and try to stop them from getting away in the spaceships," Biffy replied.

Robbie said, "But searching about all those fields could take forever."

Biffy's reply was never heard because the world suddenly and unexpectedly exploded with a mighty *bang!*

***

After Biffy crawled out from under the car bonnet that had landed on him, he looked round for the others. Robbie was snarling and growling as he tried to pull a large piece of smouldering plywood from on top of Marple, whose voice could be heard coming from under the wood.

"Hey, who put the lights out?"

With Biffy's help, Robbie managed to pull the sheet clear to reveal a fattened Marple, who, like most cats after a sudden and unexpected surprise, calmly started preening himself as if nothing had happened.

"Typical cat. We have just been blown up while hurrying to stop a lot of rocket-flying mice from taking over the planet, and you stop for a quick makeover," said Robbie, spitting out plywood.

Marple stood up and said, "Have to keep up appearances. Don't want the enemy to catch us looking scruffy." And he gave Robbie a long stare.

"Don't know why you're looking at me," said Robbie defensively.

"OK! That was obviously the diversion, which means the raid is about to start," said Biffy breathlessly.

Suddenly, over the screams and shouts of panic coming from nearby, a two-tone klaxon went off, and a shaky voice sounded from a loudspeaker.

"This is an emergency! Please evacuate this area immediately and assemble in the leisure centre car park! I repeat: All visitors and stall holders must evacuate the site and assemble in the car park!" Then it clicked off.

"Let's get clear of this bomb site! We'll head towards the churchyard," said Biffy, and they quickly trotted off eastwards along the hedge.

Chapter 19

The Diversion

A little while earlier, as Biffy and his mates were making their way down to the leisure centre, Captain Cheesecake and his diversionary squad were getting close to the village. They could hear the traffic going up and down the A371 Draycott Road, a particularly busy road that goes south to the village of Draycott. He signalled for the group to land as they approached the last hedge before the road.

"OK, mice," he said, talking into his wrist communicator, "we have to cross this busy road, but we must not be seen or the game's up and we lose the element of surprise."

The general waited a few minutes until the road seemed clear of traffic, then said, "We need to keep low and go as fast as possible, straight across the road and into the hedge on the other side." He signalled his squad to follow him. One by one, they slipped into the hedge and then at full throttle shot across the road, one after the other.

By pure luck, they had chanced upon one of those strange gaps that appear in traffic for no apparent reason. In fact, highway engineers have a special technical term for it. They call it *one of those things*.

They did not, however, go by completely unobserved. An old couple had parked their car by the verge of the road to look at their road map.

"Why don't you just ask someone for directions?" asked Gladys, who was annoyed.

"Because I don't need directions. I know exactly where we are," replied Rodger, equally annoyed.

"And where exactly is that?" asked his wife.

"Well, if there is anything interesting going on, then we are as far from it as possible," said Rodger, irately looking up from his map and seeing four Martian hover scooters whizz across the road right in front of them.

Whizzz! Whizzz! Whizzz! Whizzz!

Rodger started the car and did the quickest and neatest three-point turn of his entire life. Gladys, upon recovering from being thrown about in her seat as her husband made a manoeuvre that would have impressed the best anti-hijack trainers in the world, said breathlessly, "Rodger, what on earth are you doing?"

"We're going back to where nothing interesting happens." And he sped off as fast as he could go in the opposite direction.

The mice, of course, saw nothing of this and were regrouping on the other side of the hedge that lined the road.

"So far so good," said the captain. "We go through that hedge over there," and he pointed to the northwest, "nip over a small river, then in through some large trees, and we are there. Follow me!"

The captain zipped off with his squad following close behind. They passed over the hedge, then over the river and through the trees. The four scooters came out into the churchyard.

The layout of the old graveyard took the captain and his mice completely by surprise.

"*Arrrg, watch out!*" shouted the captain, who had narrowly avoided going head-on into a large tombstone and was now sprawled out on the grass. His scooter was sticking nose first in a nearby flower bed.

The other mice, having heard their captain shouting a warning, had slowed up and were slowly emerging from the trees. They landed near the crash site and dismounted. Meanwhile, Captain Cheesecake was brushing himself off. He said, "That was a close thing. Blooming stupid place to put a load of stones. Someone could get hurt, you know!" The other mice had managed to get his scooter out of the ground and were busy checking it over.

"Seems to be OK, only scratched the paintwork," said one of them.

"Right. We are going to hide the scooters among those trees over there." And the captain pointed to a clump of trees near the edge of the churchyard.

Once the scooters had been hidden in the trees, the mice prepared to set out on their mission to locate and blow up the BBC Radio truck.

Captain Cheesecake led his mice down to the bottom of the churchyard, which was not that far from the bottom of the sports ground.

"OK, once we have found the exact location of the BBC Radio transmitter, we will place the bomb and set off the diversion," said the captain, while rummaging about in his pockets.

He took out a small black box from his hip pocket and extended a metal aerial about 20 centimetres. Mounted on the front of the box was a dial that consisted of a small window in which a needle swung from left to right against a scale, reading from zero to maximum, this indicated the strength of the radio signal.

He pressed a switch on the side of the box, and the needle swung over to maximum for a second and then came to rest again on the zero. He looked up and said, "This radio signal locator will detect any radio signals that are coming from the BBC's outside broadcast unit."

The captain started turning about on the spot while carefully watching the needle. The needle suddenly swung across to the far side of the dial and rested on maximum. He looked up. The aerial was pointing towards the far southern end of the group of tents making up the cheese festival.

"Right, this way!" he ordered and set off towards the source of the signal. The other mice in his squad followed behind.

They carefully skirted round the bottom edge of the field, the captain keeping a careful watch on his radio detector. They were almost running out of field when the needle swung back to zero position, indicating that they had gone past the source of the radio signal.

Captain Cheesecake held up his paw to signal the squad to halt. "Hold up, I've lost the signal," said the captain, slowly twisting this way then that as he pointed it back northward towards a group of parked cars, vans, and other vehicles that were located just behind the last large tent. The needle jumped over to the full position again. "Got it," said the captain and looked up from the dial.

"Right, it's over there among all those trucks and caravans at the back of that big tent," he said, putting away the detector. "We are probably looking for something big, with some kind of dish or antennae on it," he continued, scanning the vehicle park for the radio truck.

"You mean something like that," said one of the mice who was standing next to the captain. He pointed to a large silver camper-like truck with the letters *BBC* in large letters on the side, and a very large radio dish on the roof.

"OK, Thinsqueak, front and centre," ordered the captain.

Private Thinsqueak, with his explosive backpack, carefully manoeuvred himself towards the captain. He was just thankful that he was still in one piece after the short journey from the churchyard.

Captain Cheesecake said, "Good mouse," and slapped him on the back just as the general had done.

Once the other two mice had got up from lying on the ground with their paws covering their ears, the captain said, "What are you, mice or men?" Turning towards the vehicles, he said, "Follow me," and stealthily started to make his way towards the BBC Radio truck with a very nervous Thinsqueak right behind him. The other mice came on at a noticeable distance from the ever possibly exploding Thinsqueak.

A short distance from the BBC broadcast truck, a large trailer-mounted diesel generator purred away. This provided power not only for the BBC but for most of the entire festival.

Captain Cheesecake held up his paw to signal the small column to halt. Noticing the not-so-small gap between Thinsqueak and the others, he instructed, "Hurry up, we need to have a group huddle before we start the diversion!"

This proved quite difficult because the other two mice were trying to keep as far away from Thinsqueak as possible.

The captain said, "Come on, come on, get a bit closer. I don't want to have to shout. You would think that Thinsqueak was going to explode at any minute." And he slapped Thinsqueak on the back again just to make his point.

Unfortunately, the terrified Thinsqueak heard only the words "Thinsqueak" and "explode". The other two mice were lying on the ground again, covering their ears. Looking up and noticing that Thinsqueak was still assembled in the right order, they got up and dusted themselves off again.

"Right," said the exasperated captain, and he took another small box out of a pocket. This one was silver and had a large red button on it.

"The bomb will not explode until I push this button," which he then did. This time, Thinsqueak joined the other mice in lying on the ground, covering their ears.

The captain, continued in a raised voice: "But only after I arm the device." And he turned the silver box over to reveal another switch clearly marked with the word *Arm*.

For about the fourth time that afternoon, the mice got up and dusted themselves off, thankful that there was something to dust off.

The captain, giving his men a steely look, said, "Now that that's clear, let's get on with the mission. The main force should be in place by now and waiting for us to start the diversion." He then gave his squad another steely look and continued, "That's if we can all keep standing up long enough to accomplish it!" He was almost shouting when he got to the end of this little speech.

The captain and his mice were just a few metres away from the generator. The captain pointed at the noisy generator and said, "That is what is obviously supplying power to the radio truck. See those cables? We will blow up that instead of the truck. Should make a bigger bang."

The captain then said, "OK, Thinsqueak its time, run over and stick the bomb under the generator, then get back here as quickly as possible."

Thinsqueak quickly ran over to the generator, carefully took off the backpack, then carelessly chucked the bomb under the trailer that supported the generator. He then ran as fast as he could back to the others. In fact, he was so relieved that he was no longer in danger of being blown up, that he kept on running right past the astonished captain.

He ran on and on, disappearing into the Somerset afternoon, never to be seen by any Martian mouse again, and what became of him this tale does not tell.

Captain Cheesecake and the rest of his squad watched in stunned silence as Thinsqueak disappeared into the distance. When he came to his senses, the captain said, "Right, we've no time to bother about Thinsqueak just now. We need to get to a safe distance so that we can detonate the bomb. Follow me."

He led his remaining squad back towards the edge of the field, where they could still see the generator from a distance.

"Take cover!" he ordered.

For the fifth time that day, and they hoped the last, they threw themselves to the ground and covered their ears.

The captain took out the remote detonator and carefully closed the arming switch. There was a beep. He turned it over, revealing the glowing red button that meant that the bomb was in range and ready to recieve the detonating signal. First checking to see that his mice were taking cover, he pressed the button.

Nothing happened!

The captain pressed the button again. Still nothing. By this time, the other two mice had looked up, wondering why there had been no explosion.

"Drat! Someone is going to have to go back and detonate it by hand," said the captain, his face reddening with frustration. The two mice just looked at one another.

The captain decided that dealing with this new situation was not something that he trusted anyone else with and that he would have to do sort it himself, and quickly so he said "You two stay here and cover me. I'll go back and blow the thing up using my disruptor at close range."

So Captain Cheesecake slipped back to their original position near to the generator. "Hmm, much too close for comfort, I think," he muttered to himself. Taking out his disruptor, he thought, *I can't risk this not working*, so he adjusted his ray gun's force dial to the Really Big Bang setting, which was halfway between Annihilate and You Can't Be Serious.

Taking cover behind a large stone, he looked round and took careful aim at the backpack that was sitting right underneath the middle of the generator.

"Well here goes ..." and he pressed the trigger.

A very thin, but brilliantly bright jet of green light shot from the gun and hit the backpack. The captain kept up the fire until the backpack started to glow red. Then something did happen.

There was a mighty *bang!*

The generator shot about 30 metres straight up into the air and then came down, slamming into the ground, where it exploded in a huge ball of fire and smoke. All the other trucks and caravans in the vicinity were knocked onto their sides by the explosion and set ablaze.

The BBC Radio truck was on its roof. The poor people inside were just able to get out through the smashed windows and escape to safety.

Captain Cheesecake looked up from the ditch that he had landed in when blown clear away from the explosion. When he saw the utter devastation he had caused, he said to no one in particular, "Oops, maybe that bomb was a tiny bit too big after all."

CHAPTER 20

The Raid Begins

A short time earlier, while the diversion squad were preparing to start the diversion, the general had led the main force safely across the fields and had negotiated the road. They were now at the churchyard and had hidden most of the scooters among the various trees and bushes, except for the special ones fitted out to carry the cheese back to the spaceships.

As Captain Cheesecake was trying to detonate the bomb, the general and his mice were waiting for the big bang and the resulting panic that would hopefully clear all the tents.

"Should have gone off by now," said the general to Lieutenant Fondue.

Fondue replied, "Well, we can't radio them because it might give away their position. We just have to wait and hope."

"I'm just worried that the bomb won't be big enough."

Suddenly there was a mighty *bang*, followed by a *whoosh*, then a *thump*, then the whole world exploded.

As Lieutenant Fondue looked up from where he was lying, he noticed the general lying on the ground next to him.

Both mice were covering their ears with their paws. The lieutenant gently nudged the general. When the general looked up and uncovered his ears, Fondue said, "What were you saying about the bomb not being big enough, sir?"

Suddenly, amid all the screams and shouts of panic coming from around the tents and stalls of the cheese festival, a two-toned klaxon went off, followed by the same loudspeaker message that was being heard by Biffy and his friends, who were picking themselves up from the debris at the southern end of the festival site.

"This is an emergency. Please evacuate this area immediately and assemble in the leisure centre car park! I repeat, all visitors and stall holders must evacuate the site and assemble in the car park!" Then it clicked off.

"*This is it!*" The general had to shout to be heard above all the noise coming from just the other side of the trees.

"Fondue, nip in quickly and check whether everyone has cleared the area."

The general did not see Lieutenant Fondue raising his eyebrows as he nipped past him and disappeared through the thin treeline that separated the churchyard from the exploding cheese festival. A moment later, he reappeared and said, "All clear, sir!"

"OK, each group take a tent and get as much cheese as the scooters will carry, then get back to the main landing site as quickly as possible! Don't wait to regroup. Just go!" shouted the general.

All five groups set off through the trees and went for the five biggest tents that they could see.

***

Biffy, Marple, and Robbie were getting close to the churchyard when Biffy suddenly stopped and said, "There's movement, look!" They had just spotted the mice emerging from the trees that surrounded the churchyard.

"They must have been waiting for the diversion in the churchyard," said Marple.

"Some of them seem to be riding on what looks like flying steam irons," said Robbie.

Biffy suddenly stopped again. Robbie, who nearly ran straight into him, said, "I wish you would stop doing that." But Biffy was doing some quick thinking. He was quite a bit smarter than the average cat, our Biffy.

"So most of the mice were on foot, but we know that the main landing site is a bit further away."

Robbie said "Yeah, so?"

"So they must have used those flying iron thingies to get here," replied Biffy.

"That's right, they must have hidden the other contraptions somewhere close by," said Marple, catching on to Biffy's line of thought.

"And that helps us how?" asked Robbie, who was also catching on to Biffy's line of thought, and was beginning to worry that another one of Biffy's crazy plans was being forged.

Biffy said, "OK, they must be in the churchyard. Come on!" And he rushed off with Robbie and Marple hurrying on behind.

***

Meanwhile the mice had found the tents containing the main cheese stalls.

Each group picked a tent, quickly checked that there was nobody in them, and then went in. At first, they just stood and stared in wonderment at all the cheese. Then the captains came to their senses and shouted: *"Stop gaping and start loading!"*

The general had a good look about his tent. All the tables were groaning under the weight of every type and style of cheese imaginable: huge slabs of bright orange Cheddar, great big round Edams, wedges of Brie and Camembert – in fact it was cheese heaven! He spoke into his wrist communicator to the other captains.

"OK, forget any soft stuff and stuff in tubs. Just go for smaller pieces of the harder cheese. Fill the saddlebags with as much as you can, then get out and back to the ships!"

CHAPTER 21

The Hover Scooters

Meanwhile, back in the churchyard, Biffy and Marple busily searched for the Martian mice's hidden scooters while Robbie acted as lookout from the edge of the trees.

Marple was rummaging about in a small clump of trees when he suddenly said, "Biffy, quick, they're over here!"

Biffy rushed over to where Marple's voice was coming from and found him in the middle of about a dozen of the scooters.

Just then, Robbie came rushing in, panting. "Quick, they're coming back!"

"Good, we can follow them to their main landing site," said Biffy, who was now having a close look at one of the scooters.

"But if they head off on these things, how are we going to follow them?" asked Marple.

Biffy looked up from the scooter and said, "OK they're a bit small, but I have a great idea."

"Oh no, not again!" said Robbie, alarmed.

Ignoring Robbie, Biffy said, "The controls look quite similar to a motorbike. Shouldn't be too difficult to handle."

"And how many motorbikes have you ridden lately?" asked Robbie.

"Oh come now, we handled the skateboard OK," said Biffy, with that same mad look in his eyes that he had when he decided that all three of them could ride together on a single skateboard.

"If OK means crashing into a hedge at high speed and then being squashed by a nesting cat," said Robbie testily.

"Yes, but these look a lot more controllable, and we get one each," said Biffy encouragingly.

"There is no way I am getting on one of those contraptions!" said Robbie, sitting down in a huff. If he could have folded his arms, he would have.

"They're here!" exclaimed Marple.

"OK, let's hide and watch how they operate them," said Biffy, slipping into a bush near to one of the scooters. Robbie was still muttering under his breath when Marple grabbed him and pulled him under a nearby thorn bush, just as three mice appeared.

The special cheese-carrying scooter from this squad had gone on ahead to get to the landing site as quickly as possible. The mice climbed onto their scooters. One of them was right in front of where Biffy was hiding and watching closely.

The mouse pressed a large green button that was obviously the start button, and the scooter started to emit a low, whistling hum. He then pulled a small lever about halfway down its slot. The scooter slowly rose and started to hover about 25 centimetres above the ground.

He leaned forward and took hold of the handlebars, but then suddenly straightened up again. Looking at his hip, he reached down and removed his blaster from its holster.

Biffy, Marple, and Robbie stiffened, thinking they had been discovered, but the mouse seemed to be interested only in his gun. There was a low beeping noise coming from it. Turning to his comrades he held up a paw and said, "Hold up, guys, I think my blaster is on the blink. Looks like it needs charging again." He turned a dial on it, then pointed it at an old tree stump and pressed the trigger. A thin, but very bright beam of green light shot out and hit the stump, which instantly exploded in a ball of flame. "Seems OK, must be a faulty alarm." He put it back into its holster.

As he leaned forward once more and turned the handlebars, he said, "OK, guys, let's head back to the ships." When he twisted the grip on the end of one of the handlebars, the scooter sped off out of the trees.

Once the other two mice had left, following their comrade, Biffy and his mates emerged from their hiding place. "Looks like they are much more dangerous than we thought," Biffy admitted, "but we have to follow them," and he leaped onto one of the remaining scooters, which immediately toppled over. Biffy tumbled in a pile on the ground.

"Yeh, this is going to work," commented Robbie sarcastically and raising his eyebrows.

Unperturbed, Biffy got up and righted the scooter.

"So let's try something else," said Biffy, and he pressed the green button. The scooter seemed to straighten itself and it started to hum just like the other one. Biffy jumped onto the seat. It was a bit small, with quite a few bits of Biffy not really supported by anything, but it seemed stable. Biffy sat on the Martian machine and thought, *Just as well these mice are as big as they are. I am struggling to sit on this thing as it is.* But he said, "OK, this feels more like it," and he pulled the lever right down.

"Arrrrgg!"

The scooter shot straight up into the treetops, jamming Biffy's head between the forks of a large branch.

"Don't think you were supposed to do that," said Robbie unhelpfully.

"Right, I think I have the hang of it now," said Biffy, while freeing himself from the branch. He pushed the lever back up to the top.

"Arrrrgg!"

The scooter plunged straight down, hit the ground with a thump, and toppled over again. Marple helped Biffy up. The scooter had righted itself and was sitting humming on the ground.

"OK this time," said Biffy. If he'd had sleeves, he would have been rolling them up, but instead he got onto the scooter for the third time, hopefully lucky.

He slowly pulled the lever down to about halfway. The scooter rose gently and hovered about 25 centimetres above the ground.

"See? Easy once you know how," said Biffy, greatly relieved but bruised. The other two reluctantly climbed onto their scooters and all three were soon hovering just above the ground.

"OK, we're up, but how do you make them go?" asked Marple.

"I think you twist this hand grip," replied Robbie. He twisted his sharply.

"Howwwwwl!" Robbie shot off at full speed, totally out of control, howling all the way. He disappeared through the bushes at the bottom of the churchyard and whizzed through the neighbouring caravan park.

He shot through several washing lines one after another *"Owch! Owch! Owch!"* There was an accompanying sound of clothes pegs pinging off in all directions and a shower of wet clothes, mostly landing on the roofs of the caravans parked nearby. Having narrowly avoided decapitation and now sporting an assortment of odd clothes, including three socks, a pair of blue polka dot pyjama bottoms, a bra, and a pair of frilly pink underpants that had somehow landed on his head, covering one eye and with one ear sticking out of one of the legs, he came hurtling back towards the churchyard. *"Arrrrrrgg!"*

Just as he shot through the bushes to the other side, he managed to release the grip. The scooter slowed to a stop just in front of an astonished Biffy and Marple.

"So, that's how you do it is it?" said Biffy.

"Nice bandana," said Marple with a smirk.

Robbie pulled the pants from his head and hurriedly tossed them aside, looking embarrassed.

Still smirking, Marple said, "A bit heavy on the acceleration there, Robbie mate."

"Hold up, won't the mice notice that three of their scooters are missing?" asked Robbie, looking up suddenly.

"Yeh, they might get the wind up and be on their guard for us," added Marple.

Biffy thought for a few moments then said, "OK; First, they still have no idea that anyone is on to them. Second, someone finding the scooters would take them all or cause an alarm. The fact that there has been no alarm will convince the mice that they've just been misplaced or something."

"I'm still not convinced," said Robbie.

"Well there isn't anything we can do about it, so we will just have to chance it to luck," said Biffy. "OK, let's go, and easy on that twist grip."

"Wait a minute, I'm still covered in laundry," said Robbie.

"This is no time to discuss your domestic arrangements. We've a world to save," said Biffy, and he shot off after the mice.

Marple set off after him. Looking round, he shouted back to Robbie, "Come on, there's no time to waste!"

Poor Robbie had no option but to follow his friends – socks, pyjamas, and all.

They followed the line that the mice had taken and were soon heading across country, hopefully towards the secret hiding place of the Martian spaceships.

Biffy glanced back to make sure that the others were following, He thought, *Good, they seem close enough not to lose me. Safety be dammed! We're too far behind those mice.* So he twisted round in his saddle and shouted, "Come on, we need to catch up!" Then he twisted the throttle all the way round.

"Wooooeee!" shouted Biffy as the scooter shot forward. It was just as well that he was holding on so tightly because he had been lifted right out of the saddle and was being held horizontally in the slip stream.

"Arrrrgg!" Biffy was having the white-knuckle ride of his life as he zipped at great speed across the countryside. The machine seemed to have some kind of internal guidance system as it kept narrowly avoiding low hedges, walls, and other obstacles that would soon have proved impervious to Biffy and his pals, who had also gone full throttle.

All three of them were now hanging on for life to their speeding scooters as they zipped along, darting past trees and only just clearing those low obstacles.

Although the machines were very good at avoiding those obstacles that were on the ground, they completely ignored those that were in the air. An example would be the large tree branch speeding directly towards Biffy's head.

"Arrrrg!" Biffy just managed to duck in time as he whizzed by, leaves and twigs whipping at his ears as he went. By the cries and curses coming from behind him, the other two were faring no better.

Biffy, struggling against the buffeting and jarring, managed to twist the throttle back a bit, slowing the scooter enough for him to get back into the saddle and bring it to a controlled stop.

He was just about to relax when from behind him he heard, "Watch out!"

Robbie shot past like a meteor, sending Biffy's scooter into a furious spin.

"Arrrrrrrrrrrrrrgggggggg!" shouted Biffy as the scooter spun round and round at incredible speed. After what seemed like ages to Biffy (it was actually only about fifteen seconds), the scooter's spin started to slow, and the revolving eventually stopped, but Biffy felt like his brain was still spinning round inside his head.

Meanwhile, Robbie had lost his grip and tumbled into a shallow ditch with a loud whimper. Luckily, this was filled with soft leaves which softened the blow.

Marple was last seen heading towards a large holly bush. He just managed to shout, *"Someone move that bush!"* before it seemed to swallow him and his scooter up with no noise at all except for a last *"Arrrrrrgg!"* then silence.

Biffy sat on his now stationary scooter that was hovering 25 centimetres above the ground. He pushed the lever gently up, and the machine landed softly. He gave his head a shake to try and get rid of the remaining giddiness and slowly got off and looked about.

Robbie was climbing out of the ditch, still sporting his collected washwear. His scooter, which had gone back to hover mode once he released the throttle, hovered nearby. Marple was nowhere to be seen.

Robbie waddled unsteadily up to Biffy and said, "I think I will walk the rest of the way, if you don't mind."

Biffy just grunted and said, "Where's Marple?"

A disembodied voice floated down out of the holly tree. "I'm up here."

Biffy and Robbie walked over to the source of the voice and looked up into the holly's branches.

"What is it about you and bird's-nests?" asked Robbie.

Marple had ended up in an old crow's nest. He looked down at his friends and said, "At least this one is a bit more stable. *Arrrrrgg!*"

Down came Marple, nest and all. This time, however, Robbie, having learned not to stand under nesting cats, got clear in time.

Disentangling himself from the remains of the nest and picking bits of twig and feathers from his fur, Marple said thoughtfully, "We need to review our transport policy."

CHAPTER 22

Biffy Strikes Back

As Biffy, Marple, and Robbie took stock of their situation, the three of them started to giggle a bit, the way you do sometimes after a scary but exciting event. They were brought to their senses by the distant sound of more scooters.

"Shh!" said Biffy, and they all hid in the cover of the holly bush.

Four more scooters loaded with stolen cheese whizzed by and disappeared through the line of trees that lay just in front of their hiding place.

"Come on," said Biffy, hightailing it for the treeline with Marple and Robbie coming on behind. They crept through the trees and looked out into the field beyond. There were six tall rocket-shaped spaceships sitting on their tail fins in the field just the beyond the trees. "This is it, the main landing site," said Biffy excitedly.

"How many mice do you think were left to guard the ships?" asked Robbie quietly.

"No way of knowing at this stage. We need more information," whispered Biffy.

Meanwhile the mice had landed next to one of the tall rocket ships. It looked as if they were about to start unpacking the scooter's saddlebags. Another mouse appeared at the top of a ladder that led from an open airlock that was located just above where the tail fins joined the hull of the spaceship.

The mouse quickly descended the ladder and said something that Biffy could not hear. The mice got back onto their scooters and shot off towards another of the spaceships.

This particular spaceship was a lot nearer the treeline than the others. The shining nameplate could be clearly seen. It was the *Zulupapalulu*. The flagship was to be loaded first.

Meanwhile the three mice that Biffy and his friends had watched to find out how to operate the scooters and then followed to the secret landing site had joined up with their comrade on the special scooter. They had already unloaded their cheese at the flagship and were now heading back to the raid to get more cheese.

The newly arrived mice landed next to the ship's ladder, where they started to unpack the saddlebags of their precious cargo. They carefully placed the stolen cheese in a neat pile and then secured it, using what looked like bungee cords similar to those that people use to tie stuff to car roof racks.

"We need to get a bit closer," said Biffy, and he crept along the treeline. The others followed him in silence, and they quickly came to within earshot of the mice, who had just unpacked the cheese.

A mouse appeared at the rocket ship's airlock and shouted down to the mice at the bottom. "Hold up, guys!" He then quickly descended the ladder Once at the bottom He then said, "OK, the general wants everyone except the crew of the flagship to join the raid in order to get more cheese. You will have to lead them to the site. Bengy and I can load this stuff into the ship."

Mice started to appear at the airlocks of the other five rockets, two from each. They quickly descended the ladders and went round to the opposite side of the ships from the airlock.

Looking on, Biffy whispered, "Now we know the answer to your question, Robbie. There would have been twelve of them."

"Yeh, but it looks as though they're all going to hightail it back to the cheese festival," said Marple.

"That leaves just the two guarding this ship here," said Biffy, still whispering so they wouldn't give away their position.

The other mice were by now lowering the remaining hover scooters using what looked like lorry tailgate lifts that descended from another hatch in the back of the ships. Then they mounted up and followed the lead mice out through the trees and away to the raid.

The mouse left by the flagship ladder was admiring the large pile of delicious cheese.

Biffy turned to his friends. "Right, this is the opportunity we have been waiting for. There is only one of them."

Just then, another mouse appeared in the airlock and started to descend the ladder.

"OK, there are only *two* of them," corrected Biffy. "But we still have the advantage of overwhelming number superiority and the element of surprise."

"Yeah, but remember they have those ray guns," said Robbie.

"Hey, that's right. They did look rather dangerous," agreed Marple.

Biffy thought for few seconds and then said, "We still have the element of surprise, and they are far too busy with all that cheese to notice us if we sneak up on them and pounce quickly."

"Sounds like a plan," said Marple.

Robbie said, "I'm not sure I fancy getting fried by a cheese-happy mouse with a ray gun."

"Neither do I, mate," agreed Marple.

"Look, no one is going to get fried. Their guns are in their holsters, and they have no idea what's coming."

"And what exactly is coming?" asked Robbie, beginning to notice that mad look on Biffy's face again.

"Me!" said Biffy, and he set off at once, creeping along on his belly towards the unsuspecting mouse. Marple got the idea and went after the other one, creeping round so he could approach from the rear.

Biffy had managed to creep stealthily right up to the mouse in front of him. Robbie, who was still standing in stunned silence, watched in amazement as Biffy stopped and sat up right behind the mouse.

Just then, the other mouse looked up and saw Biffy sitting right behind his comrade. His eyes went wide with surprise and terror. He tried to say something but could only open and close his mouth.

The other mouse, the one about to find out what was coming, looked at him and said, "What's up with you? You would think you'd just seen a cat or something!"

Just then, Biffy cleared his throat loudly and said, "Meow!"

The mouse stopped and turned round very slowly. When he saw Biffy, he just froze in terror.

Biffy said, "Say cheese."

Whack!

The mouse landed in an unconscious pile on the ground. The other mouse tried to escape up the ladder, but a well-aimed lump of cheddar caught him on the back of the head, and he toppled unconscious in a pile at the foot of the ladder.

"Nice throw, Robbie. Well, that was a piece of cake!" said Biffy.

"Don't you mean cheese?" said Marple, giggling.

Robbie had now joined them and said, "You're stark raving bonkers, you know that, don't you, Biffy?"

"That was a bit mad, now that you think about it," said Marple.

"Gets the job done," Biffy said happily.

"Well the job's not finished yet. What do we do now?" asked Robbie.

Biffy thought for a few moments before saying, "The others will be returning with more cheese soon. In the meanwhile, we can try and delay their departure."

"OK, and how do we do that?" asked Robbie.

"No idea," replied Biffy.

"Well that's a help," said Robbie.

Marple, who had been nosing about the bottom of the spaceship, said, "This must be the rocket engine." He was pointing to several short, blackened funnels. The funnels narrowed at the top and became short tubes that disappeared into the bottom of the spaceship.

Robbie's face suddenly widened into a smile. Running up to the rocket's exhaust cones, his tail wagging like mad, he said, "Quick, stuff that cheese into the end of those tubes!"

"Now who's completely bonkers?" said Biffy, looking puzzled.

"No, no," said Robbie in earnest. "I remember hearing one of my humans say once that some kid had stuffed a banana up his car's exhaust pipe. The engine would not start. It took him hours to locate the problem."

"Great idea, Robbie, let's get to it," enthused Biffy.

Biffy, Marple, and Robbie got to work. First they had to untie the bungees. Biffy stood for a few moments, thoughtfully twisting and stretching one, before dropping it with the others. They then started breaking the cheese into manageable lumps that they carried to the bottom of the spaceship where they started sticking large lumps of Cheddar, Gouda, and Gorgonzola into the Martian spaceship's rocket tubes. "Wow, this stuff stinks," commented Robbie.

"Yeah, but it tastes delicious," said Marple, licking his paws in between chunks.

"Stop eating and keep stuffing," ordered Biffy. "Hopefully it will slow them down a bit."

It took Biffy, Marple, and Robbie less than half an hour to stuff as much cheese as they could into the *Zulupapalulu's* rocket tubes.

"There's still quite a lot of this Cheddar left," said Robbie, looking at the small yet not insubstantial pile of cheese sitting on the ground.

Biffy seemed lost in thought again. He said softly as if thinking out loud: "Cheddar saved by Cheddar," and he gave a little chuckle.

"You feeling all right?" asked Marple.

Biffy looked up. "What? Yes, yes, just thinking."

"You worry me, you know that don't you, Biffy mate?" said Robbie anxiously.

Biffy just smiled his Cheshire cat smile and said, "Good," though unlike Lewis Carol's Cheshire cat, he did not disappear, leaving just the smile.

The very visible Biffy then said, "Right, the other mice will be returning soon with more stolen cheese."

"We probably don't have enough time or cheese to disable the rest of the rockets," said Marple.

"No need. I have a cunning plan," said Biffy, mysteriously.

"Oh no!" said Robbie.

CHAPTER 23

Another Crazy Plan

Marple was mumbling something and counting on his claws. He looked up and said, "Well, we have accounted for two of the mice, so I reckon that that leaves about a couple of dozen at least left for us to deal with."

"Bit of a tall order that," said Robbie.

Biffy said nothing but was thinking quickly, looking at the remaining cheese and remembering how effective it had been in stunning that second mouse. Then he looked at the bungee cords lying piled on the ground. Finally he looked up and said, "What if we could knock a good number of them out of the air as they come in?"

Although Biffy had already announced that he had another cunning plan, Robbie knew that he was just dying for someone to ask him what it was, so he obligingly said, "How do we do that, then?"

Getting into his stride, Biffy began to explain. "So, we know how effective a large chunk of well-aimed cheddar is. We just need to be able to throw it farther and faster."

"Great idea. How?" asked Robbie.

"Well, that's just the trick, isn't it?" said Biffy.

"What hare-brained scheme for getting us killed have you got now?" enquired Robbie.

Biffy was starting to get that mad look again. He said, "Robbie, do you remember where you left those bits of laundry that you got covered in?"

"Yeah. There – over there," said Robbie, pointing back through the treeline, where they had left their commandeered scooters.

"There was a bra, wasn't there?" asked Biffy.

"Was there? I was too busy not getting killed to notice," replied Robbie.

"Quick, go and have a look and bring it back here. You go with him Marple. Those mice can't be far away."

While Robbie and Marple nipped off to find the discarded laundry, Biffy went and picked up one of the bungee cords that the mice had used to secure the cheese and was giving it a few more experimental twists and stretches.

He murmured to himself, "Yes, a couple of these will do nicely. I just hope we have enough time for this to work."

Marple and Robbie came back through the trees, with Robbie carrying the special garment in his teeth. He dropped it at Biffy's feet and said, "Come on then, out with it. What's this brilliant plan that's going to try and get us killed again?"

"Oh you of little faith, none of my plans so far have been that dangerous, have they?" asked Biffy.

"Yes," replied Marple and Robbie together.

"Well, there's no glory and trumpets without a little danger, eh?" and having said that, Biffy gathered up the bungees and walked over to the trees. As he was walking, he looked back around and said "Bring the bra."

"You've still not told us what we are going to do," said Marple.

"Two things," said Biffy. "First, we are going to build a catapult using the bra cup and a couple of these bungees. We can knock them off as they appear through the trees."

"There are an awful lot of them for one catapult," interjected Robbie.

"And that's where number two comes in. We are going to set up a line of tripwires between some of the trees using the remaining cords."

"But the scooters are in the air," said Robbie.

"Yes, the bungees will have to be set at mouse chest height."

"There's no way we have enough to cover the entire treeline!" exclaimed Marple.

"I know," said Biffy, "We can only cover every second tree pair and hope we catch a few coming in unawares. Remember, this should all come as a big surprise to them."

Biffy took a good look along the line of trees that ran along the southern edge of the field to where it turned and ran back westward again.

"I don't think that they will head for the far corner of the field, so we can start about two trees in," said Biffy as he hurriedly carried the bungees towards where the treeline turned at the corner of the field. The whole treeline formed a square that surrounded the entire field, hiding the spaceships from general view.

Biffy, Marple, and Robbie got to work stretching bungees between the selected trees. Luckily the bungees were long enough to stretch between the trees with enough spare to tie them round the tree trunks.

Biffy handed one end of a bungee to Robbie, who took the bungee firmly between his teeth and suddenly started growling and tugging and shaking his head from side to side, wagging his tail like mad.

"Robbie!" shouted Biffy. "You're doing it again."

Robbie stopped and dropped the bungee. Shrugging his shoulders and looking really embarrassed, he said, "Sorry, forgot where I was again. I do love a game of tug-o-war."

"Time and place, Robbie. Time and place," said Biffy scornfully.

"Sorry," said Robbie, now looking down at his feet.

"Never mind," said Biffy and patted Robbie on the shoulders. "Come on, let's get this done, yes?"

"OK," said Robbie, looking up and wagging his tail again.

The tripwires were soon all in place. Biffy checked each one to make sure that they were at the correct height and tight enough to unseat any mouse that hit them.

"We need to use the catapult against the mice that get past the tripwires," said Biffy.

"You still haven't told us how you're going to construct a catapult," said Robbie, "This is not *Blue Peter*, you know. You can't just say 'Here's one I made earlier' and pull it from behind a bush."

"You'll see. Come on." And Biffy led them back through the trees into the landing field.

Marple whispered to Robbie, "I don't think he knows. He's just winging it."

"I heard that," said Biffy.

"Look, Biffy mate. We're running out of time. The mice will probably be returning at any minute," said Marple.

"Exactly, good of you to volunteer."

"What?" said a surprised Marple.

"We need a lookout to tell us when the mice are coming," said Biffy.

"Yes, and …?" said Marple, really beginning to worry now.

"Well, since you seem to enjoy nesting like a bird, you can climb up that tree and whistle if you see anything."

"Wait a minute now. I haven't climbed trees since I was a kitten," entreated Marple.

Robbie was enjoying the fact that it was not him being asked to do something mad and dangerous for a change.

"Come on, Marple, you've been up two today already. Third time lucky, eh?" said Biffy, who pointed at one of the trees not far from the first tripwire. "Up you go."

Marple opened his mouth to say something but then just closed it again. He thought instead, *Oh well, probably safer up there than down here.* Of course he was dead wrong.

While Marple was making a fairly decent job of climbing up the tree to act as lookout, Biffy and Robbie were looking about the field for something to help them build the catapult.

"We need couple of small trees quite close together or a couple of fence posts or something," said Biffy.

"How about those old gate posts?" said Robbie.

"What old gate posts?" asked Biffy.

"Those old gate posts in the middle of the field," answered Robbie pointing to two old but sturdy-looking gate posts.

"Perfect!" exclaimed Biffy as he rushed over to examine them.

"Quick, go fetch the remaining bungees and that bra."

As Robbie shot off back through the trees Biffy got to work designing the catapult in his head, he was wondering why they called it a *cat-a-pult*. He was soon to find out.

Robbie returned carrying two bungees and the old bra. Biffy got to work disassembling the bra and attaching one end of a bungee to each side of the bra cup, which now hung suspended between the two bungees. "Quick, tie one end to that gate post. We need to have this thing as taut as possible," said Biffy as he took the other end and stretched it towards the other post about two metres away.

Robbie, however, did not have a tight enough hold on his end and it sprang out of his paws. There was a loud whack!

"*Ouch!*" yelled Biffy, who was now lying face down in the muck with the bra cup over his head. "You idiot! Try and be more careful!" he shouted, getting up with the bra still on his head.

"Well, we know that it will be effective," said Robbie.

"How's that, then?" asked Biffy, pulling the bra from his head.

"Well, if it can knock you over without even being loaded, what's a kilogram of cheddar at full pelt going to do?"

"Good point. Let's go and get what's left of the cheese and try this baby out," said Biffy excitedly.

Once they were back with as much of the cheddar as they could carry, they reconnected the catapult bungees to the gate posts and made them really tight.

"OK, load her up," ordered Biffy.

Robbie took a large lump of cheddar about the size of a grapefruit and placed it into the bra cup. Biffy took up the cup and aimed it at one of the trees that was supporting the first tripwire. He was able to adjust his aim by pulling slightly left or right. Trembling under the strain, Biffy had pulled the *launcher*, as he had decided to call it, back as far as he could. Taking careful aim, he was just about to let go when his footing slipped and he lost his aim.

Twang!

"*Arrrrgg!*" screamed Biffy as he was catapulted, along with the cheese, high into the air.

"Arrrrgg!" Biffy continued to scream as he headed directly for Marple, sitting high in his tree, acting as lookout.

"Arrrrgg!" screamed Marple, who had just twisted round to whistle a warning when he saw a large piece of cheddar accompanied by a large tabby cat flying directly towards him. Luckily, the cheese missed. Unluckily, Biffy didn't.

Whack!

Biffy knocked Marple clear off his branch, and the two of them crashed onto a nearby pine tree, where they continued their descent by crashing down through its branches.

"Ouch! Ow! Ouch! Ow! Ouch!"

Luckily, their fall was broken about halfway down by a large – yes, you guessed it – bird's-nest.

Robbie rushed over to see if they were all right. Looking up into the tree, he spotted his two friends and said, "You know, Biffy, that nesting thing seems to be catching."

Peering over the rim of the nest, Marple said, "At least this one definitely seems a bit more stable."

No sooner had Marple uttered those words than there was a mighty *crack!*

Biffy and Marple plummeted towards the ground, surrounded by the debris of the definitely less-than-stable bird's-nest. Just before he hit the ground, Marple thought soulfully, *Why is it always me?*

Crunch! Biffy and Marple hit the ground.

"Ouch!" said Biffy.

"Ouch!" said Marple.

Biffy got up, rubbing his sore and bruised behind, and said, "Well, the catapult works. We just need to improve our aim."

Marple said, "That's good because they're coming!"

CHAPTER 24

The Battle of Cheddar

"Quick, let's get back to the catapult," ordered Biffy, running off towards their makeshift artillery, followed quickly by Marple and Robbie. They soon got to work loading the makeshift catapult with a large chunk of cheese and preparing to fire their first round in the coming battle.

As the mice approached the treeline, they separated into their original rocket groups and sped on, totally oblivious of any potential calamity.

One of the mice shouted as he neared the treeline, "Way hay, nearly there! Mars, here we come. *Oomf!*"

"Arrrrgg!"

"Ouch!"

"Sqeaaaaak!"

Four of the scooter riders were knocked flying as their machines crashed into the unseen tripwires. Their scooters shot through the treeline riderless then slowed to a stop just beyond the trees and just sat hovering in the air.

But one scooter passed through one of the unprotected spaces between the trees. The mouse slowed right down and looked behind him to see what all the commotion was.

Whack!

"Great shot!" said Robbie, quickly reloading the catapult. An excellently aimed piece of cheddar had sent the mouse flying.

The next line of mice had seen what had happened immediately in front of them, but they were going too fast and were too close to the first line of scooters to react. The Martian mice had obviously never read the highway code section about safe stopping distances.

Once again, four of the riders were knocked off by the tripwires, but a fifth got through one of the unprotected spaces.

Whack!

Another well-aimed cheese cannonball sent him flying.

"OK, so far so good," said Biffy, "but we have lost the surprise element by now."

"Yes, it's going to start getting interesting," said Marple. The third line of scooters started to take avoiding action.

Crunch!

One mouse had swerved to avoid hitting the tripwire and hit a tree instead.

Crash!

Two others actually collided, knocking each other off.

Whack!

One scooter rider managed to fly over the bungee cord but then got knocked off by a low branch.

Whack!

The third successful hit by the catapult sent flying the only mouse from the third group to get through the trees.

By now the fourth group of scooters had slowed right down and were slowly approaching the treeline. Picking the clear spaces, they slipped cautiously through, into the field beyond.

Whack!

The catapult found its fourth victim and sent the mouse flying. The remaining mice brought their scooters to a sudden halt. One of them said, "What the heck!" and turned round towards the source of the attack.

Whack!

A large lump of cheddar sent him flying.

One mouse got his blaster out and managed a wild shot at Biffy and his friends before succumbing to the catapult's deadly aim.

Riderless scooters lay abandoned all over the place, and the mice were running about in all directions, squeaking in terror as lumps of cheddar flew with deadly accuracy through the air. Meanwhile, Marple added to the mice's terror by leaping out from behind things, teeth bared, hissing and screeching at full voice.

"Meowwwwww!"

Marple was having the time of his life chasing terrified mice all over the field and helping create a sense of panic and chaos among them.

Mice started to shoot wildly at anything that moved. The air was full of bright green light beams. One hit an abandoned scooter that exploded in a ball of flame. Another hit a scooter that was flying directly at Biffy. It veered off, trailing smoke. The mouse flying it managed to jump clear just before it hit one of the rockets, ricocheted off, and exploded in the air.

The general, who had just emerged from the trees, took one look at the chaotic battle scene and screamed into his wrist communicator, "Cease fire! Cease fire!" Then in a slightly calmer voice he said, "The rockets are too close to use our blasters."

He had just finished that last sentence when a wild disruptor beam, which had been fired by a mouse running full pelt for one of the rockets and was firing blindly in all directions as he ran, just missed him.

"Cease fire, drat it!" he bellowed.

"All mice are to retreat to the rockets," he ordered. "I repeat, retreat immediately to the ships."

The mice all started to run helter-skelter for the ships. Once inside, they did not wait for further orders. As soon as a rocket had a full crew on board they just blasted off for home.

In fact, rockets started blasting off all over the place. The general, Lieutenant Fondue, and the rest of the crew of the *Zulupapalulu* had made it safely to the flagship. As soon as the general reached the bridge, he asked Space Pilot Stilton for a full report on the current situation.

"Sir, the other ships have skedaddled," said the pilot.

"What?" shouted the enraged general. "I'll have the cowards shot when I get back to Mars."

"What do we do now, General?" asked Lieutenant Fondue.

"We need to get back to the far side of the moon so that we can regroup and plan our next move," said the general as he turned to face Space Pilot Stilton.

"OK, Stilton, get us out of here fast."

"Aye, aye, General," replied the pilot as he started to manipulate the controls that would fire the *Zulupapalulu*'s rocket motors and launch the ship. He finally hit the big red start button.

There was a brief roar followed by a few short rasping coughs, a wet splutter, and a final soft sigh before everything went silent again. "Err, I think there may be something wrong with the engine," muttered the pilot.

The general's face went all purple, and he shouted, "What?"

The pilot, who was now looking very alarmed, said, "I can't get the rockets to start."

"Well check the engineering computer and find out what's wrong," commanded the furious general.

"Yes, sir, at once, sir." The pilot turned to his control console, and while carefully monitoring his computer screen, he started punching up display charts and images. Lieutenant Fondue went over to help diagnose the problem. After a few moments, the lieutenant looked up and said to the general, "Looks like something is blocking the rocket tubes. Someone will have to go outside and unblock them."

The whole crew looked up at the general with rather scared expressions on their faces. "If you want a job done well, do it yourself," said the general, pulling his blaster from his holster and heading for the hatch of the main airlock.

Lieutenant Fondue took a few paces forward. "General, are you crazy? Those cats are still out there."

The general paused and turned to face his crew. "A good general should never expect his soldiers to do anything that he wouldn't." He then turned and hit the hatch open button, stepped into the airlock, and said, "Close the hatch behind me." The pilot hit the close button, and the hatch slid shut with a mechanical whirring sound, ending in a final-sounding clunk.

The general lifted his wrist communicator to his mouth and pressed the call button. The radio crackled into life. "Fondue here, sir."

"OK, I'm going out. Open the outer hatch."

"Yes, sir." The lieutenant ordered the pilot to open the outer hatch.

There was that same mechanical whirring noise as the hatch opened and a short ladder extended down to the ground. The general stood just inside the hatchway and looked around the immediate area of the ship. There seemed to be no sign of the cats and dog, so he turned and stepped quickly down the ladder.

As soon as he had reached the bottom, he brought up his blaster and took off the safety lock. "Right, I will soon sort out any of those pesky cats if they are still about," he said to himself as he crept down and under the tail fins of the ship towards the rocket tubes in the centre. He could see large pieces of Gorgonzola sticking out of the bottom of the tubes. "Holy Emmental!" he said out loud and pressed the call buttonon his communicator. Fondue answered at once. "Yes, sir, Fondue here."

"Those feline devils have stuffed the rocket tubes with cheese. I'm going to try and dislodge it using my disruptor. You should be able to tell on the monitor when it's clear."

"Yes, sir, I will call you once the computer tells us the tubes are clear."

Lifting his disruptor and turning the force dial to the Cheese setting, which was halfway between Annihilate and Tickle, he pointed the muzzle towards the cheese-stuffed tubes and pressed the trigger. A jet of green light shot out and hit the cheese sticking out of the rockets. At first nothing seemed to be happening. Then slowly the cheese started to tremble slightly, then bubble, and then at last it started to run and drop out of the tubes.

After ten minutes or so the tubes looked clear, so the general stopped firing and carefully approached the pile of bubbling cheese that had formed beneath the rocket tubes. He stepped under the central tube and looked up.

Splat!

A large glob of melted cheese hit him square in the face. "Oh flipping squeak," said the general angrily, wiping the greasy mess from his eyes.

At that moment the call buzzer on the general's communicator buzzed. He pressed the answer stud, and an excited-sounding Fondue, almost shouting, said, "Sir, it's worked. The tubes are clear, and we have a green light for blast off."

"Praise the Gouda!" said the general. "I'm coming back on board. Get ready to launch as soon as the outer hatch is closed."

"Yes, sir," replied the lieutenant.

Chapter 25

What Martian Mice Are Made Of

No sooner had the general put his paw on the first run of the ladder than he heard a commotion behind him.

"Quick, he's getting away!" shouted Marple.

"I'll get him," said Robbie.

"No," said Biffy "This time I need to end this once and for all."

Fondue's almost hysterical voice came over the communicator. "Quick, General, get back inside! Those pesky cats are back."

The general stepped down from the ladder and turned to face his enemies. Fondue's hysterical voice came back over the communicator again. "General! What in the name of all the cheese are you doing?"

General Squeakcheesy replied, "I'm going to show those cats just what we Martian mice are made of." Those words were going to go down in history as rather unfortunate but true. The general lifted his wrist communicator up to his mouth and said, "Fondue, once I have dealt with these oversized puff balls I'll get back inside and we can take off."

The general lifted up his blaster menacingly and advanced towards Biffy, who was also advancing towards the gun-totting mouse.

"That's far enough," said Biffy. The two were only about a dozen paces apart.

The general pointed his disruptor right between Biffy's eyes and said "OK, you over stuffed bag of cream, this is the mouse who caught the cat" and he pressed the trigger of his blaster.

Biffy had been priming himself, and all his cat instincts and natural self-preservation skills came into play instantly. With one of his few remaining nine lives hanging in the balance, and just as the general touched his trigger, Biffy sprang. A jet of green light caught the end of his tail as he disappeared into the air and came down with a nasty squelch right on top of the unfortunate general. When Biffy got up, the whole world could certainly see what Martian mice are made of.

Suddenly there was a roar and a blast of heat as the *Zulupapalulu* blasted off, never to be seen by anyone on Earth again.

Biffy picked himself up from where he had been blown over by the rocket blast and said, "Well, I think we've seen the last of them."

Marple said "Hey, do you think any of those scooter things are still working? Be a quick way home."

"There is no way I am ever getting back on one of those things," declared Robbie.

"Yes, this time you are probably right, it's time for a nice quiet stroll back home for tea, boys."

So without looking back at the chaotic scene behind them, Biffy, Marple, and Robbie left the field of the Battle of Cheddar and strolled off home as if nothing had ever happened.

Chapter 26

Sardines for Tea

Biffy's owner, Mrs Pat Ferguson, was standing in the open kitchen doorway, shouting for him: "Biffy, come on, puss. Biffy, dinner time!"

Biffy, walking as casually as possible, appeared round the corner of the house and sat down in front of her. He gave a quick swish of his tail and meowed pathetically. She looked down at Biffy and said, "Where have you been all day? Sleeping under the rhododendrons again? What a lazy cat you are!" She then turned and went into the kitchen. Biffy followed, meowing.

"I suppose you want your favourite? Sardines," she said with a smile.

Biffy dutifully swished his tail and licked his chops expectantly.

She went to the cupboard and brought out a tin of sardines, which she took over to the kitchen table. Biffy followed, meowing all the time. Well, it was what was expected of him. When he heard the tin being opened, he jumped up, patting her skirt playfully.

She bent down and tipped the fish into Biffy's food bowl. "There you are, though you don't deserve it." Biffy was too busy eating to comment.

Mrs Ferguson just shook her head and said, "You know, Biffy, I think I saw a mouse last night. What do you think we keep you for?" Biffy said nothing and just kept eating the delicious sardines. Mrs Ferguson sighed and bent down to scratch Biffy behind the ears. "If a fleet of Martian mice landed today and tried to steal all the cheese, we certainly could not rely on you to stop them, could we?"

Biffy thought, Huh, that's all she knows. Still I am looking forward to a nice quiet life without any further adventures.

Of course he was dead wrong.

The End